Finding HER

Siri's Heart
Books 1 & 2

AMAZON BESTSELLING AUTHOR
JESSIKA KLIDE

Copyright © 2017 Jessika Klide, LLC

This is a work of fiction. Names, characters, places, brands, media, events and incidents are either the product of the author's imagination or are used fictitiously. Any similarities to actual events and persons, living or dead, are purely coincidental. Any trademarks, service marks, product names, named features, artists and bands are assumed to be the property of their respective owners, and are used for reference and without permission. The publication / use of these trademarks is not authorized, associated with, or sponsored by the trademark owners. There is no implied endorsement if any of these terms are used.

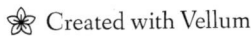 Created with Vellum

NOVELS BY JESSIKA KLIDE

Siri's Heart Book Series

Finding HER (#1 & 2)

Meeting HER (#3)

Deceiving HER (#4)

Denying HER (#5)

Choosing HER (#6)

Saving HER (#7)

Doubting HER (#8)

Taming HER (#9)

Claiming HER (#10)

Losing HER (#11)

The End of HER (#12)

Capturing HER (#13) - Coming Soon

Standalones

Donut Dilemma

I Hope You Dance

Sam, I Am

Falling For His Badass - Coming Next

Holiday Novellas

Zane, A Scrooged Christmas

Siri's Heart is dedicated to my husband, my soulmate, my Golden God. Without his forever love, this book series would never have been written. I am eternally grateful for his love and devotion. He continues to inspire me.

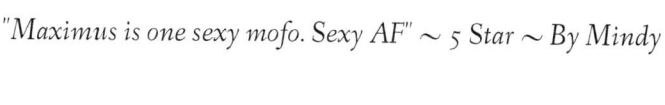

"Maximus is one sexy mofo. Sexy AF" ~ 5 Star ~ By Mindy

"Siri is so uniquely special, beautiful inside and out, strong, passionate." ~ 5 Star ~ by Erotic Romance Book Blog with Sandy

"I said it before and I'll say it again. This series is a brilliant piece of writing magic! Thank you Jessika for giving us this outstanding series!" ~ 5 Star ~ by Cynthia Hughes

"I am invested in these characters and I can't wait to get more of them. I am grateful to be a part of their world!" ~ 5 Star ~ By A. Branch

FINDING HER

Finding Her is the prelude to Siri's Heart, a torrid love affair between the dancing diva, **Siri Wright,** and the dazzling, but driven young entrepreneur, **Maximus Aurelius Moore.**

Book 1: ***Hard-Core***

Am I really hardcore? You bet I am! I sound like a conceited, son of a ... but the brutal hardcore truth is ...

I am that good! I leave 'em wanting more of Moore.

Book 2: ***Seary***

When Aurei travels to Las Vegas to scout a new investment opportunity, a dancer named Seary, he finds a woman who makes him feel alive. Determined to have a relationship with her, he sets about a bold plan of action to make the elusive star his exclusive lover.

A NOTE FROM JESSIKA KLIDE

Because Siri Wright is a dancer, there are songs sprinkled throughout her story. They have been chosen specifically, not only for their music, but also for their lyrics, which are governed by strict copyright laws restricting the use in books.

It is certainly not necessary to listen to the music to enjoy Siri's Heart, but if you choose to, you will enhance your enjoyment, and have a fuller, deeper understanding of Siri's heart.

All playlists for Siri's Heart can be found here Youtube.com/jessikaklide in the order they appear in the stories.

May you find a love

you cannot live without!

— JESSIKA KLIDE

Everyone has secrets

— SIRI WRIGHT

CHAPTER ONE

Maximus Aurelius Moore

"Standing outside on the balcony of my Italian studio in Rome wearing only a pair of black Calvin Klein briefs, I rub my cock absentmindedly and try to wait patiently for the sweet little piece of ass I've hired to photograph to get ready for the shoot. It's been too long between visits.

Listening to the sounds of the civilized city beyond, my mind drifts back to the call I received this morning from Dirk Sam, my old army buddy. "Moore, my man! You still walking around with a dick stiff enough to be mistaken for the cyclic?"

I laughed into the phone. "I am. You still hanging a dick long enough to choke a gorilla?"

"I still don't know about that, brother, but it's longer than a banana."

"Sup, Sam-I-am? It's good to hear your voice. It's been too damn long since you needed a favor. What can I do for you?"

He chuckled into the phone. "I've got TDY orders for Rucker and wanted to hit you up for a place to stay."

"Beautiful. I'll clean off the couch. When?"

"In the spring. I'm waiting on a class assignment so I don't have the exact dates yet, but I won't be sleeping on your couch this time. I'll need a nice apartment."

"Really? A cheap scape like you never turned down a free place to crash before."

"Moore, I got hitched." Dirk laughed.

"What the fuck? Hitched as in married?" I asked truly shocked.

"Yeah. Married. Me." Dirk laughed even harder. "It's a long story, bro. Too long for a phone call. It'll take several six-packs of brew to get through."

"With news like this, you gotta give me the short version."

"I fucked this crazy bitch years ago in London and when I came back, I looked her up. She needed a husband, so I married her." He chuckled enjoying stringing me along.

"You're fucking with me, Sam." I laughed.

"No, man. I'm serious. I'm not pulling a fast one over on you. I'm for real. I've made a deal with a devil, but she's one helluva devil." He paused, then asked. "So, can you help me find an apartment?"

"Of course. No problem. Just let me know as soon as you know what your dates are and I'll lock you into a lease. You'll be all set when you arrive."

"Great. I knew I could count on you."

"Always, brother. I got your back."

He put his hand over the phone to muffle the sound of his voice. "My buddy stationed at Fort Rucker.... Yeah. Don't worry. He'll find us a place that's not in the slums...." He

"s a place that's not in the slums...." He removes his hand and I hear the crazy British she-devil.

"You trust this buddy?"

"With my life."

"Good, because if you drag me to a hellhole to live, I'll kill you, Nicholas Dirkerus Sam."

I start to laugh hearing Dirk's life being threaten so easily, but so effectively. "I'll stock the fridge with a case of beer. This story is going to be good." I tell him.

"Yeah." He laughs with me. "It is a good one."

"Babe." He tells the Brit. "Chillax! Go do what you do. I got this." Then he tells me in a loud whisper. "Make it a really nice one."

"You got it. I know just the place. A new, gated community."

"Thanks, Hard. I'll be in touch."

A car horn on the street below brings me back to the balcony. I glance down to see a man shaking his fist out of the window of his Fiat.

I smirk, then laugh, remembering the nickname Sam-I-am tagged me with. It's been a long time since I was called Hard, but some names just stick and that's one of those names.

Army Aviation Flight School, Fort Rucker, Alabama. Six years earlier.

Dirk bragged to the others on the flight line Monday morning.

"Dudes, my wingman Moore earned a new nickname Saturday night."

"Spill it!"

"His new name is Hard-Core, but I call him Hard for short."

They all laughed at that. "Cause his dick stays hard all the time?"

"Hey Hard, come over here and tell them what happened Saturday night."

"Naw man. Let it lay."

"Hell no!" They all chimed in. "Spill it!"

"We walk in, right? And immediately, Ole Hulk here draws the ladies' eyes. You can hear the word 'Eye Candy' buzzing around the bar."

"That's two words, Sam."

"Shut the fuck up, Moore! Anyway, we sit down at a table and nothing happens, right? Wrong! Some drunk chick comes up, plops down in his lap and starts to grind him."

"No, she didn't. Quit exaggerating."

"Yes, she fucking did. But our Officer and a Gentleman here, being the best damn wingman ever, simply stands up and excuses himself to the restroom leaving me the drunk chica. When he comes back, I've done made a move to hold her right here." He pointed to his dick and they all laughed. *"But her wing-lady rescues her from my evil cock, and they leave."* He frowned and everyone boos. *"Which should be bad, right? Wrong! That's good because she broke the ice and now Mr. Muscles here is acting like a fucking chick magnet. I swear they were swarming."* He flexed his biceps. *"Maybe I should improve my guns."*

Everyone laughed.

"By the time midnight rolls around, there is sure 'nough a catfight brewing as the pussies positioned themselves to make a play for my main man. While I'm here working my ass off to pick one up, he's working hard over there not to have a threesome at the table."

"So how did he get the new nickname, Hard-Core?"

"Patience. I'm getting to that!"

"Did he go hardcore on them and fuck those pussies like the dawg we know he is?"

Someone chanted. "Who let the dawg out?" So, everyone barked.

"Naw man! He mows them down! It was brutal, I tell you!" He hung his head then shook it. "He told them. 'Look! I'm not into you and I'm not getting "in" to you.'"

"Ahhhh!" They all moaned.

"That's a hardcore rejection right there."

I laugh. It'll be good to see ole Sam-I-am again. The first time I laid eyes on Dirk Sam, we were asked to stand at the Hail and Farewell party and were introduced as the only two bachelors in Green Flight. Sitting at opposite ends of the same table, we stood locking eyes and sizing each other up. We were both athletic specimens at 6' tall and around 220 pounds, but I was wearing a J-Crew shirt with khakis and he faded distressed jeans with a t-shirt that read Loose Cannon. I'm blonde and with a beach tan. He's a dark brunette with olive skin.

To everyone there we looked like opposites, but not to me. He had the same look in his eye.

"Aurelius is the youngest candidate too."

All eyes turned to the dark haired, dark eyed young man, and the moment Dirk realized their eyes were on him instead of me, the blonde buck with the crooked grin, he quickly set the record straight, calling the crowd out with a wise-guy grin of his own. "I hope you ladies and gentlemen did not just profile this dark meat as the Mafioso because I'm Dirk Sam. He's Aurelius Moore."

Dirk was enjoying the hell out of pushing their politically correct buttons and I knew we would be brothers. I gave him a heads-up man salute and simply said to the crowd. "Ciao."

From that point on, the practical jokes and the antics were nonstop. If we weren't pushing each other's buttons, we were teaming up to push everyone else's.

I lean over the balcony railing and spit. Then a crooked grin slides on at the fond memory that simple action conjures. The seed spitting contest was one of the best. Vodka filled watermelons produced quite a show. First place was hard to earn, but Hard-Core and Sam I am prevailed.

CHAPTER TWO

I stand, then stretch. Sam and I were made from the same mold, just handed two different lives. Sam told me during one late night of drinking while we were closing down the local bar. "I joined the military because I had nowhere else to go. My mother died a week after I graduated from high school." He hung his head and I listened quietly, knowing it was difficult for him to share. "At 18, I was homeless. Going through her stuff, I came across newspaper clippings of this British politician that looked like a real prick. Part of me wondered what the hell she had these for, but the other part knew. He was my sperm donor." He looked up at me and smirked. "I took the last money I had and bought a plane ticket to London. 'Blimey Bastard'" He looked down the bar for a long time into his distant past. I could tell something had happened that he wasn't going to share. When he looked back at me, he had pushed the memory down deep inside. "I almost got myself killed. I hightailed it back to the States, and joined the Army to fly this badass bird." He grinned and downed the beer. That was the last he spoke of his hardships and he never mentioned London again until the other day. I wonder what happened to send him back to London? And now he's married and to a crazy British bitch? Can't wait to hear that wild tale."

I enlisted not because I had to, but rather because I wanted to. Flying Apache helicopters just appealed to me. When my dad retired from the military, he moved us back home close to his parents in rural Alabama. I fell in love with the warbirds flying overhead. The sound their blades make as they chop the air overhead. Nothing else like it. But I did rush into enlisting when I was featured on the cover of an Italian tabloid. "Maximus Moore, Rising Star on the Italian Social Scene. Perhaps we should consider this young American, inline to inherit the Liotine Fortune, as the most eligible young bachelor in Italy. We will definitely be keeping a watchful eye on him." That comment sent me straight to the recruiter without thinking twice and without telling a soul. I signed away 6 years of my life determined to be who I am, not who someone else portrayed me to be.

I drop my head and smirk. Man did that announcement cause an uproar.

We were all at the family villa in Italy, on spring break, when Grandpa Al said to me. "Maximus, I would like for you to come to Italy when you finish high school to discuss your future."

I raised my head then turned my eyes to his. "This is as good a time as any, I reckon, to tell y'all." Pushing my chair back, I stood to face him and the rest of them, proudly announcing my decision. "I've enlisted in the Army. I'll be leaving the day after graduation for basic training. I'm going to fly Apaches."

The air seemed to have been sucked out of the room. Grandpa Al was the first to speak. "Maximus, what have you done?"

"I've done what I wanted to do. I want to serve my country and I want to fly helicopters. Grandpa, I'm not university material. I don't think I can stomach four more years of school to earn a boring degree, doing something I will loathe. I can go through Warrant Officer Candidate School then flight school in less than a year and come out a helicopter pilot."

Grandpa looked right at my mom and said. "Zita, you and Bob should have told him."

"Should have told me what?" I asked her. She sighed, didn't answer, and looked at my dad. He simply shrugged his shoulders, then spoke for them. "Son, when you were young your Grandpa here established a trust fund in your name. We didn't want you to grow up using it as a crutch. We wanted to make you an independent thinker. We were going to tell you after you graduated."

"That's dope!" I beamed at everyone. "Thanks, Grandpa!" His stern face made me falter and I looked at my mom and dad for more information.

"It transferred when you turned 18," Bob answered my unasked question.

I turned back to Grandpa Al. He told me. "There is a million-dollars in it."

"Whoa," was all I could say.

If I had known, I wouldn't have enlisted and my life would certainly not have become the big complicated collection of secrets it is.

Grandpa spent every waking moment with me those two weeks, giving me a crash course in business management and investing. "Maximus, use your talents. You have a good head on your shoulders. Begin buying other businesses and learn from them. Hire go-getters. Treat them with respect. Pay them well. Reward good effort. Do not hesitate to use the talents of your employees. Remember your family loves you. They will be loyal to you and want you to succeed. Be loyal to your employees in return, but allow no one to mind your business but yourself."

As it turns out, Grandpa was right. My personality, coupled with a logical mind and the concise communication skills I learned in the military has made me a keen observer and an excellent venture capitalist. I've managed to turn that million-dollar trust fund into Maximus Enterprises, a multimillion-dollar conglomeration of successful business ventures worth multi-millions.

I turn my ear to the door, listening for the model, but I hear only silence. She must be applying makeup. I should have told her to stay natural. I lift my face to the sun and let my mind drift along, waiting patiently.

Maintaining a dual lifestyle has been challenging, to say the least, but I've successfully kept my business persona and my American life separate with the help of a successful team of handpicked Italian family members I employ. Back home in Alabama, my homeboys know I have money, but not the extent of it. My military family doesn't know anything at all. They simply know me as Warrant Officer Aurei Moore, an Alabama homeboy, currently stationed at Fort Rucker.

I lace my fingers, put my hands on top of my head and chuckle. I've got jaw-dropping news for Sam I am too. If he comes in after my military obligation ends this spring and I have officially resigned, I'm going to come out of the millionaire player closet. My bro is going to be shocked. I chuckle harder as my eyes follow a car passing on the street below.

CHAPTER THREE

"Signore?" The sweet little piece of ass calls looking for me from deep inside the studio. I twist my head to her voice. Her bare feet pad across the hardwood floor as she comes closer then stops in the doorway. "Why are you in the cold air?"

"Reminds me how alive I am."

"Are you crazy man? It's freezing!"

"I laugh. I guess I am a crazy man standing out here freezing my balls blue. I shift my stance to look into the room. Her arms are crossed over her nakedness and she is obviously cold.

"I will wear the mink." She says and retreats inside. I smile at her sweet little ass as she disappears.

Granny Moore introduced me to the art of photography when I was a preteen. She was worried about my 'badass' attitude and gave me my first camera. "You seem to be finding yourself in the middle of schoolyard battles, Dear. You should report Ann's bullying to the teachers. Let the adults handle the children."

I didn't answer. I knew the only way to protect my little sister was to kick their asses and since I could, I did. Worked too. But then the next year, we moved to another school, and it started all over again, so I had to teach those bullies too.

"You are breeding anger, and anger breeds unhappiness, and unhappiness isn't a pretty sight for these old eyes." She told me as she handed me a box wrapped in Superman gift paper. I smile again remembering her underlying message. She was proud of me for doing the right thing, even though it wasn't what she wanted me to do. "I want you to take this and look for positive things to fill you. Focus on the inherent beauty in this world. It is everywhere. Do that, Hun, for your Granny Moore and your life will be full of warmth and goodness."

That summer, I came to Italy to stay with the Liotine side of my family. I took that camera and found beautiful girls willing to pose topless for me. I smirk, remembering. My life has definitely been full of warmth and goodness. I turn my ear to the door, listening, but there is still silence. When this last model arrived, I told her like I've told all the others before her. "I'm sure Adona informed you, but I want to be clear before we begin. I shoot nudes. You aren't required to do anything you don't want to do. Are we clear?"

"Sì. Where do I change?"

I didn't answer. I pointed to the spot where she was standing, then to the fur coats hanging on the hook, and left the room for the balcony.

Adona's Modeling Agency has been providing me with a steady stream of beautiful women to photograph and thereby fuck for years. Since modeling is such a cut throat industry the girls wouldn't dream of dishing amongst themselves about fucking the photographer for fear of being backstabbed nor would they brag about it for fear of being fired or blackballed. Which allows me to fuck with no strings attached whenever I want, and I can have a new one every time. It's perfect for someone in my position. My only requirement of Adona is the models she chooses for me are single and my identity remains anonymous.

Today's beauty steps back up to the doorway wearing

the sable mink now. Lowering my head, turning my ear to the door, I wait for her to join me, but she doesn't. Instead, I hear her feet retreat inside to the warmth of the heated floor.

"Are you ready?" I ask over my shoulder.

"Sì. I am ready." Her tone is professional, but enticing. "Please come here, Americano. Where it is warm."

I turn to face the room and see her hovering at the edge of the shadow. Should I hold my hand out and ask her to come to me? The sun is bright and I might be able to capture the colors in her raven hair. Inside it will simply blend with the black mink she has chosen to wear. Unless I turn the spotlights on, but I don't feel like dealing with setting them up now. I walk the few steps to the door, lift my arms overhead, brace on the threshold and lean in, watching her reaction to me and trying to decide inside or outside.

The sweet little piece of ass takes a step closer, coming out of the shadow, throws open the fur coat and invitingly strikes a perfect nude pose. My cock thumps with her uninhibited presentation, making me grin at her in appreciation while noticing how her pale skin illuminates in the direct sunlight. My decision is made. Although her hair would shine in the sun, it would drain her pallor skin of color. Inside it is. Taking the camera hanging on the door latch, I put it around my neck and up to my eye, turn it on her and focus the lens. Her nakedness shines white and pasty against the darkness of the mink. Her hair mixing with it forms a hood effect around her heart shaped face. Snapping pictures of her, I get right to work.

After a few dozen full-length ones, I lower the lens to capture her breasts.

I love a good set of tits. I fell head over heels for a perfect pair thanks to a scene from my childhood of Lynda Carter as Wonder Woman running on the beach in an old TV rerun. Her natural D's bouncing up and down so hypnotically, moving and flowing. They gave me my first hard-on and my first ejaculation, so naturally, I'm an expert on the subject, and although I fuck skinny models whose tits are not natural, but rather the best implants money can buy, I'm still a connoisseur. She's a perfect C cup with soft pink nipples that face forward for the most part and are only slightly off center. I zoom in on the tips which are shrunken tight by the exposure to the cold air in her bare-all offering. Tiny goosebumps are raised in the areola and my cock starts to come alive. She arches her back, pushing her breasts out and turns slightly to give me the best angle, then she dips her knees, pushes her ass out working the angles for me. She's a pro and I do appreciate pros. I shoot a trail of zoomed shots, lower. Her skin is flawless. No moles, no freckles. Her navel sits in a concave stomach. She's a tad too skinny. She could use a little meat on her bones. I drop the camera down to find her ... 'runway' of pubic hair. I zoom the focus in tight and see her pink flesh peeking through the hair. Although I love a beautiful pair of tits, pussy is what I really have a thing for. Ah. There's the prize. My dick thumps at the sight, hardening further. It's been too long between fucks. I click off dozens of pictures. Moving around her, dropping lower and shooting an up angle, testing her comfort level with my focus to find she doesn't shy away. She continues to offer different poses and lets me work whatever area I want. She is comfortable in her skin. When I stand up straight and zoom out, turning the focus on her face, I find her smiling, then she winks, flirting.

I smile behind the camera. Good. This session won't last long. She's already thinking of sex.

CHAPTER FOUR

I zoom in on her smile and her lips. Bright white teeth against ruby red lipstick. She bites her lower lip and pulls, slowly letting the teeth slip off. An imp. She could be fun. I can see the bare color of her real lips at the bite mark. Too much lipstick. Not kissable yet. I move up to her painted eyes. Her eyeshadow is lighter shades of browns. She has the standard heavy sable eyeliner and false lashes attached. Her eye color is not surprising. A thought pops into my brain and I drop the camera, pondering the words that flashed by. Boring brown, I prefer blue or green eyed blondes.

She drops her professional pose, letting the mink coat fall and stands straight looking concerned. "What is wrong?" Her fingers feel her false lashes to make sure they are intact. "My eyes?"

"No. They are good." I answer but she doesn't buy it. High dollar models are worth their price because they read the photographer's body language and feed off them. She's not going to let it go. She saw my lack of interest, but I don't want to tell her that her eyes are a boring brown.

"What then?" She gives me a searching look and her expression says, 'bull shit, you lost focus' and I know I can't get away without an adequate answer, so I stall while I search for a truthful, yet tactful reason.

"Nothing. You're good. You are doing fine."

Her hands find her hips and her lips pout. High price models are also high strung and can be complete drama queens given the right push. I don't want to push those buttons, so I tell her, the rest of the truth that struck me and hope it is enough to avoid a scene. "I just decided to, ah, you know, do a blonde later." I lift the camera to hide behind it and encourage her to continue. Please.... No drama....

I see her pouting lips change to pursed lips as she tilts her head and digests this information. Circling around her again, clicking pictures of her expressions, I feed her ego with her truth. "Your sable hair shines with the sheen of a raven's coat, blending with the color of the black mink, perfectly framing your beautiful, exquisite face. Your pale skin is flawless. Turn this way now." I start to instruct her, knowing I must take command of the photo shoot and demand her compliance.

"Grazie." She smiles, pleased with my compliments, turns for me, then after a little while offers a flirt. "You are, ah, pretending I am blonde, no?"

I grin from behind the camera. We are going to have fun together. "Am I?"

"Sì. You are." She states as fact, so I lower the camera to look directly into her imp eyes.

"Really?"

She gives me a flirtatious smirk and nods at my briefs.

I glance down and see my bulging cock.

"You are Mister Big Man, no?"

Mister Big Man. That's a new one. "Hahaha." I laugh out loud, then give her a direct piercing look with the same flirtatious smile. "No. Not yet."

Her flirtatious smirk falters, and her eyes flare shocked. "Dio buono, che diventa più grande?"

Time to play. I laugh again, reach for her hand, then pull her with me to the bar. "Let's have a drink." When we get there, I take the camera off and set it down. "Sì, my cock gets bigger."

"Hai capito Italiana?" She sputters, a little embarrassed that I understood her outburst

"Sì, parlo correntemente l' Italiano." She rolls her eyes. Busted.

I take a crystal canister filled with amber alcohol and pop the seal, turn the lone glass over and pour myself a stiff one. "Your English is good, but needs practice. Will you drink with me?"

"What kind?" She leans over and examines the bottle.

"Crown Royal. It's Canadian whiskey. Smooth."

"Whiskey. Umm. Sì, a small one."

"Good girl." Leaning over to open the cabinet door, I reach inside and get another lowball glass. "Would you like it on the rocks?" I glance back at her and catch her eyeing my ass with a look that says 'that's an incredible ass.' Standing back up, I finish my question. "Or neat?"

"Pardon? I do not understand."

"On the rocks means over ice, and neat means straight from the bottle."

She looks at my glass and says. "Neat, please."

Pouring her a full shot, I ask. "Will you need water to chase it?"

"Not if it is good whiskey." She answers and when I hand it to her she swirls the contents and sniffs the liquid. "Umm." She lifts her shot and we clink our glasses together. There is no hesitation or timidness to her consumption. She tosses it back like a veteran. "Ummhmm. Good whiskey, no?"

I smile and reach for her glass. "Another?"

"Sì, please."

As I fill our glasses for round two, I feel her eyes on my ass again. I smirk to myself, knowing she is trying to maintain a level of professionalism, but can't help enjoying the view. When I turn around and extend her glass, I ask. "Do you like a man's ass?" I smirk at her confused face, then again clink our glasses, and drink alone.

She frowns at me."Pardon? I do not understand."

"Do you like a man's ass?" I ask again.

"Mansass? I do not know this term." She looks at her drink.

Unable to hide my amusement, I chuckle, but don't offer an explanation. Instead, I let my eyes devour hers.

When she begins to get uncomfortable, I ask again not taking my eyes off hers as I put my fingers under her arm and lift the glass to her lips. "Do you like a man's ass?"

She stares into mine and I can see the desire building in hers. When the glass reaches her lips, she drops them to drink. I know the burning sensation she feels as the liquid slides down her throat then lights a fire in her gut, colliding with the passion I churned in her pussy. When she swallows, I ease the pressure of my fingers and let the glass gently lower from her lips. When our eyes connect again, I see the fire is lit and before I remove my fingers from her arm, I rub her skin with my thumb. Sending the signal that I may be demanding, but I am an excellent lover. The smile has left her face and the laughter gone from her eyes. Sliding my fingers down her forearm to her hand, I gently remove the empty glass. I set it down on the bar without looking and bring her hand to my lips. I place a small kiss on the back, and her eyes fall to my mouth, watching my lips. When I pull back, I whisper, knowing she has forgotten my question. "Do you?" I can see her about to nod yes and smile at her willingness to capitulate so easily. "Like a man's ... ass?" I emphasize ass, making her blink then think.

She frowns and says. "Ass ... is ... donkey, no?"

I give her a playful grin, take the hand I hold and put it on my ass, then squeeze her fingers, grabbing a handful of my butt cheek. "No. Do you like a." I emphasize the last two words, dragging them out. "Man's ... ass?"

She laughs freely. "Oh. Hahaha." And I am rewarded with her true beauty as it bursts forth. "Sì." She tells me enthusiastically. "I do. I like a man's ass." She gives it another soft squeeze and I laugh with her, then step back and turn to the bar once more. Without asking, I turn to pour us another drink.

CHAPTER FIVE

She stands beside me and lays her hand on my arm. "My English friend says arse." As the liquid splashes in the glasses, she continues. "Mister Very Big Man has a very big ass, no?"

I chuckle and agree as we prepare to toss it down. "Yes he does and he is glad you like it."

"Umm hmm." She grins back at me flirting. "It is very good, no?"

"So I've been told." We clink and drink, then I pick up the camera and wave her away. "Practice your English. Where are you from?" She walks around the studio, admiring the photos on the walls and answering my questions. "How long have you lived in Rome? How many siblings do you have? How were you discovered? How long have you been modeling? Do you enjoy it? What's your last project? What country do you like the most?" I must help her a few times find the correct translation and we laugh at her mispronunciations. When her English is almost perfect, I zoom in for a tight shot of her face and I ask the one question that I really want answered honestly. Ready to catch her expression, hoping to capture the moment of perfection. "Have you been in love?"

"Sì." She grins a sexy grin.

"Are you in love now?"

"Sì." She looks directly into the camera.

I sigh, knowing the photo opportunity is a bust. Her smile turns seductive and she walks over, so I lower the camera, and look her eye to eye. She slides up against me, and I feel the cool skin of her hand, followed by the tickle of the fur as she touches my side, then slides it around and down inside my briefs to rest on my ass. She whispers up at me. "I am in love now." That's not what I wanted to hear. "Will we fuck, Mister Very Big Man with the very big ass?" That's what I wanted to hear.

I grin down on her. "Do you want to fuck?"

She leans her head back and smiles up at me. "Sì. I want to fuck a very big man with a very big ass. Do you want to fuck?" She kneads my butt cheek.

"I want to fuck too." I lean down, nuzzle her ear and she leans into me. I remove her hand from my ass and hold it as I whisper. "But first." I lean away and search her eyes. They tell me she is willing to do whatever I ask so I command her in a soft, hushed voice. "Walk to the door." I nod my head at the balcony door. "Go." She backs away to do as I ask, bringing my hand with her. I pull her back to me, bringing her hand to my lips once more, place a soft kiss again on it, and say. "Go and wait for me."

Her smile is sweet before she saunters off. As soon as she turns her back, I push my briefs down, kick them off, lean my bare ass against the bar and cross my legs at the ankle. My cock stands out like a flag pole. Raising the camera, I'm ready to begin snapping pictures again. When she reaches the door, she spins around and sees my posture, the camera and my flag pole. A wide, happy smile breaks across her face. The sound of the shutter clicking echoes between us as she drops the fur without being told, letting it slide slowly down her body, softly, silently, spilling onto the floor and laying in a pile around her feet.

"Perfect." I compliment her. "Now tease me," I command again.

She begins to strike sexy poses, showing off her skill. She is a veteran and works her modeling magic as she moves back to me. Hair up, then down. Arms out then in. Legs straight. Hips cocked. Tits hidden, then exposed. Pushed up, then flattened. When she arrives, she throws a lock of hair off her shoulder and licks her tongue across her lips, teasing me with the tip. She drags her manicured nails down the groove in my abs and asks in a sultry voice. "What is your name, Mister Very Big Man?"

I watch the wet, pink tip of her tongue play with her lips and I can almost taste the sweetness of her pink little clit. "Hard." I tell her honestly.

Her laugh is husky, but flirty. "You are Mister, Very Big, Very Hard Man, no?" She drags the tips of her fingers down to my cock and sends shivers down to my balls, making them draw up and tighten. "What is your name, please?"

"Hard-Core." My voice is husky and my tongue touches the corner of my mouth.

She giggles softly, tilting her face up to mine, knowing she is getting to me. "How did you get such a wonderful name?" She pulls her fingertips from the base of my cock to the tip.

Her light touch makes it thump, and my balls begin to fill with semen. I wet my lips, letting my tongue slide across while my hands clench, grabbing empty air so I can keep them out of her hair while she plays this game of tease with me. Her hand wraps itself around my shaft and she slides it to the base, gripping my cock tight. She raises her eyebrows at me, silently beckoning the answer.

"An Army bro."

She looks surprised by my answer, then drops my cock and takes a step back. I almost growl and grab her, but her concerned expression stops me. Her eyebrows meet in the middle, almost forming a unibrow and she looks completely upset. "Army bro? You are gay man?"

The ridiculousness of that makes me laugh out loud. My hands unclench, and reach for her as I say. "Hell no!"

She falls into my arms, giggling, then I hear my southern accent repeated back to me with a thick

Italian accent. "Hell no!" She leans back so she can wag her finger at me. "I teased you good, yes?"

I laugh hard again. "Yes. You teased me good."

Her face drops onto my shoulder as she laughs and I feel her shoulders shaking with the silly giggles. When the laughter finally fades away, she kisses my shoulder, and I know she has become aware of my fully hard, very large, erection pressing against her. When she looks up at me, the serious look of lust has fallen over her face. Passionate eyes, no longer boring brown.

I notice a stray strand of her hair stuck in her lipstick as she tells me sweetly. "You are a very beautiful man." I gently pull the strand off, then trace my finger along her lips. The lipstick clings to my skin and pulls her lip taut.

"We need to clean this off first."

Her reaction surprises me. She frowns slightly as she looks away, then she steps back and looks down at my cock. Her bottom lip rolls in and her teeth press down on it. I study her expression, then bend over and pick my briefs up. Taking her back into my arms, pressing her body tight against my erection, I hug it firmly between us, and put my fingers under her chin to lift her face to mine.

"I like my women natural," I whisper softly as I clean the lipstick off her lips with my briefs. "I didn't mean a blowjob, Hun."

Sheer relief falls on her face, and it makes me chuckle.

Some women just don't like to give head.

CHAPTER SIX

My phone vibrates and a groan escapes my lips, as I open my eyes to stare blankly at the ceiling. Only a handful of people have this phone number, so I know it's important and I need to at least see who is trying to contact me. The device moves on the nightstand again. "Ugh." I rub my face, taking a few seconds to clear the cobwebs.

I hear the even breathing of the woman lying next to me. Her softly exhaled breath confirms she is in a state of deep, peaceful, satisfied sleep. Glancing at her blissful expression, I gently pull my arm out from under the pillow, trying not to disturb her. She doesn't twitch and that fact makes me smirk. She called my name last night and didn't even know it. I chuckle softly.

I started off sliding my cock in slow and steady. Letting her get used to the size, as I reached around and played with her tits. When I turned up my fucking intensity, I also placed my fingers on top of her clit. Both of my hands and all my fingers working her erogenous zones, lightly tickling them. Pinching her nipple as I crushed her clit with each forward pump, then with each withdrawal returning to my dual massage. Typically, this technique, along with my sheer cock size gives an immediate orgasm, but this girl didn't give me any signs of a growing need to cum, much less an explosion. Having fucked a lot of women, I know not all of them can have orgasms. Some have physical issues that prevent it, poor souls. I was a tad disappointed because she was fun up till now and a nice distraction. But if she was one of those unfortunate women with a dead pussy, there was no point in trying to please her. No man can fuck life into a lost cause, so I set about satisfying my own needs. When she screamed at the top of her lungs, it broke my fucking trance and I was terrified my distracted hammering had been too hard. I threw her forward onto the bed, yanking my cock out and knelt frozen over her, watching her writhe.

She lifted her face off the bed and cut her eyes back at me, then sucked air in. "Per favore." Her voice sounded desperate.

"It's ok. It's ok."

She screamed. "Uuuuhhhh!" As she dropped her head and panted loud. Her breath labored.

I scanned her body, but there weren't any obvious signs that she was injured, but then again there wouldn't be, so I asked her. "Are you ok?"

"Uuuuhhhh!" She didn't answer. She shook her head violently from side to side, then beat the bed with her fist.

I leaned over to comfort her. My semi-erect cock slid harmlessly between her thighs. My lips touched the skin of her shoulder. My hips brushed her exposed ass. My touch made her scream again.

"Per favore." She reached between my legs, and smacked my cock. It wedged in a crevice, making her squirm. I gripped her hips holding her still, not wanting to hurt her again. She grunted and grabbed my balls. "Ooooooo. Ooooooo. Ooooooo." I panicked, knowing she could do real harm to me. I grabbed a hand full of her dark hair and yanked her head back. Her grip tightened like a vice.

With a voice, as cold as steel, I told her. "Drop 'em."

She let go immediately and as soon as my jewels were

free, my assets retreated out of reach. Pushing her still writhing body face down on the bed, I laid on her. Pinning her down letting the full weight of my body control her, I used her hair to turn her face to mine so I could stare into her eyes. I was astonished at the look of sheer desperation that stared back at me.

"Tell me what is wrong!" I commanded her.

She spat in my face, pushing garbled words out. "Continua ad andare. Per favore. Di Più! Di Più!"

I chuckled, relieved. "I thought.... No.... Never mind."

Her reaction to my words caught me off guard. She let out a string of muffled cuss words, then she buried her face in the covers and started to shake. "No? Ugh!" Then more cussing.

I kissed her shoulder and stroked her hair. "Shush now. Shush. Calm down. I'm going to give you what you want."

She froze and lifted her head to stare at me. I smiled. "Let me know when you are ready to continue. I'm going to give you the fucking of a lifetime."

"Continua ad andare? Per favore? Di Più?" Her eyes were big as saucers.

I laughed. "Yes, Ma'am. I can fuck all night."

She pushed up on her elbows and her eyes hunted my cock. When they rested on it, a grin broke out on her face. She rolled her eyes and collapsed on the bed, thanking the gods that I had not had a premature ejaculation.

I grabbed the extra pillows, tossed them to the foot of the bed, then picked her up and walked around to the footboard. I gave her lips a quick kiss, then turned her to face the bed. Next, I took the pillows and stuffed them between her hips and the footboard, pushed her over them and stepped up tight behind her, letting my erection press against her ass. I bent over her and nibbled the skin on her back as my hands massaged and rubbed her ass. "Comfortable?"

"Si."

"You sure you want more?" I teased her ass with my cock.

Her voice was sultry when she answered. "Si! More." Her hands reached around to her ass and she spread her butt cheeks, giving me clear access. "Fuck me, Mister Very Big Man. Fuck me hard. Hard as you can."

I placed my cock at the entrance of her begging pussy, then gripped her shoulders. My thumbs stroked circles against her skin. "Ready?" I asked her.

"Si! Hard."

Most women say that want it hard, but what they really mean is a firm thrust that bottoms out and lifts them off their toes. They want that deep g-spot that they don't know they have massaged. That or they mean hard as in fast and furious. They do not mean as hard as I can fuck because I can fuck hard, but if I did fuck as hard as I can, I would crush them. I'm a semi-pro fucker who prides myself on my skill and technique. I like to watch them lose their shit over and over before I lose mine. Then I like to do it again and again, harder and harder, until they pass out from the pleasure I have given them. That's my passion. Pleasing pussy. I may not feel the passionate love that other men feel or the level of lust that drives men to do stupid shit, but I do love women and I love satisfying them.

Since I was already giving her the good stuff before when I brought her to that near orgasmic pinnacle, and she screamed, I figured I would give her the same sex technique now, then push her over the edge with a fast finish. I thrust deep inside her, pushing her up against the pillows, lifting her off her toes, then pumped and pounded her fast. The sound her ass made smacking my groin, mixed with her moans as I brought her to the edge, sounded so sexy and I pushed her over the top like the fucking expert I am. She fell forward, trying to collapse, but I didn't let her. Oh no. That girl almost lost her mind earlier from sexual frustration, and she asked for more from me. She wanted Moore, and by God, that was exactly what I gave her. More fucking from fucking Moore! I pulled her body off the bed, squatted down and sat her on my cock, then thrust her up in the air, making her bounce on my dick. The slamming sensation she got, sent her climaxing again. When she finished, she fell forward and I eased her off, draped her again over the footboard and eased in slow. I fucked her then at my own pace and right before I blew my wad, she had another mind-blowing orgasm from my swollen size. I know it was mind-blowing cause she was moaning like a porn star.

Round one was done, then we moved to round two.

CHAPTER SEVEN

My phone starts to dance on the table again. Oh, yeah. I better get that. Leaning on my elbow, I reach for it and peek at the screen to see who the text is from. There's an iMessage from Darren Martin, a longtime friend, and venture capital partner. Sliding the screen open, I read the entire text. *Aurei, call me when you have ten minutes to talk. No rush, but today is better than tomorrow.* And later is better than sooner. Collapsing into the pillows, I pull one under my head, then I enjoy the view of the beauty's chest rise and fall. She's serene laying here with her dark hair tousled, spilling over the white pillowcase. I trace my finger down her back, then give her ass a little squeeze. She was a good fuck. Had a lot of stamina. Challenged me. I liked being pushed to perform. She rolls away, not interested in anything but sleep, and snuggles with her pillow. I grin and roll onto my back to stretch. My hand touches the top of the headboard, and I feel my camera strap. Rolling over, I drag my body over the sheets to peer down between the headboard and the mattress. It's wedged between them. How the hell did it end up there? No telling. She lost her frustration in round one, her inhibitions in round two and in round three, we were exploring all kinds of different positions.

Pulling it out, I sit up and bring it to my eye to focus, then turn it on my subject, snap the last couple of photographs of her shoot, capturing the peacefulness of the moment. Knowing it won't last, I sigh and lower it to hold in my lap. Flipping through the pics, I scan the photos. I got some good action shots and a few perfect "O" faces. I smirk. Wish I could have captured her 'Oh my god, you want me to suck that big cock?' face. That would have been priceless. I chuckle. She turned out to be an exceptionally fun fuck. I'll need to make sure to tell Adona.

The need to piss asserts itself so I set the camera on the nightstand next to my phone, then toss the covers over her nakedness, and bend down to pick up the used condoms from the floor. Her phone is lying next to them. I toss it on the nightstand too, then go to the bathroom to relieve my bladder and brush my teeth.

When I come back out, I go the bar, grab a water, then pull up a chair to hydrate while I wait for her to wake, dreading the next part.

She was fun and as much as I would love to say the words, "Let's do it again." I can't. That would be a lie, and I'm not a liar. I sit in silence just watching her breathe, knowing the sad reality of my truth is that I don't do repeats. I twist the top off the bottle of water and take a swig. It would be so nice if I could just say, 'You were a great fuck and I really enjoyed myself. Thanks. Ciao.' Shake her hand, give each other a hug and leave with smiles plastered across our faces, but that never happens. I put the top back on and stare at her without seeing her. They always want to see me again. What can I say? I smirk. I'm not just a good fuck. I'm a good fucker. The whole package. I fuck their minds too. Seduction is a true art form. Augustus taught me that. I twist the top off, take several long swallows, then put the top back on. I've had to hone my skill, not having the luxury of time. I smirk again. They don't even realize I've begun their seduction the moment they enter the studio. I learned quick that it isn't always what you say, but what you do, that makes a woman feel special and works magic on her. Getting inside her head, penetrating her mind, caressing her there, letting her feel you deep inside her subconscious, playing with her, then calling out her wild side. All the while your body language is dominating her from a safe distance, demanding her attention, but not overwhelming her with your power. Slowly giving her a little taste of that power, but not commanding her yet. Umm hmm. I love that. Nothing is more satisfying than watching them melt before you. When you start touching, commanding, tasting them, their wildness purrs, and that's when you start taming them.

That's a powerful drug! The look in their eyes when they have reached their limit, the way their bodies wither under you, needing what only you can give them. A screaming orgasm in both their head and their cunt, from your brain and your cock. Ummm. Ain't nothing better than that.

I twist the top off the water bottle, and drink half, and put it back on. Fuck! I sound like a cocky, son of a bitch. But the brutal, hardcore truth is …. I am that good. That's the real reason why they get all bent out of shape when they want to see me again and I tell them I don't. I stare at the raven-haired beauty in the bed, then drain the water bottle and resist the temptation to squeeze it, knowing the noise would wake her. I twirl the empty bottle around in my fingers instead.

Even though I'm alright with the fucking setup I have,

it doesn't mean I'm not lonely and wouldn't enjoy a steady relationship, but I've always known I'm different and finding someone different like me, is so far off the charts of possible, even a Vegas gambler wouldn't take those odds. I've never felt that undeniable spark that drives a man to hookup with one woman in a steady, long term relationship. I thought I did the first summer I discovered fucking. I hooked up with a girl whose name I can't even remember now. I banged and banged and banged her, then banged her some more. I grin. I thought I was in love, but I wasn't even in lust. I was just a horny teenage boy with an amped up sex drive, who was in love with fucking. When she returned to college, I returned to middle school and moved on. At first, I tried the whole dating scene and that was a fiasco. The drama was off the charts and with no banging to ease the pain.

I chuckle, remembering a conversation I had with my sister, Ann. "What's wrong with answering, 'Hell yeah!' when she asks me, 'Does my ass look big in these pants?' That was a fucking compliment. Not an insult." Ann started laughing and I got pissed off. "What? It was. She has a big ass and it's great!"

"Aurei, girls want it curved."

"That's fucking right! I want her ass curved too!"

"No, no."

"Yes, yes!"

"No, Bro. They want the truth curved, not straight line like that."

"What the fuck are you talking about?"

"Girls want you to tell them. 'Your ass is perfect.'"

"I did!"

"No. You told her that her ass was huge!" She rolled off the bed laughing at me.

"It is!" Now I'm laughing too.

"Girls want you to lie to them with the same lies they are telling themselves."

I stopped laughing and thought about that. "Fuck that shit! I ain't no damn liar."

"Well, you don't have to lie really, just learn her language."

I gave her a classic 'what the fuck does that mean' look.

She dies laughing again. "Just never tell another woman as long as you live that their ass looks big and you'll be ok."

"Ok, but if she wants to know how it looks in those pants what do I say?"

"Just tell her, her ass is perfect."

"THAT I can do!"

"We'll work on your curved delivery later."

I flipped her off and walked out, then tossed over my shoulder. "I ain't lying!"

I could hear her feet running at me. I braced myself and caught her as she jumped on my back. She dared me. "Last one to the creek is a rotten egg." I threw her off and we raced to the barn, then on our horses to the creek.

I stand to pace the floor, dreading the music that I'm about to face, then her phone on the nightstand rings and she sits up, dazed. It rings again and she looks around. I watch silently as she pats the bed and asks herself in Italian where her phone is.

Hair messy, makeup runny, she looks radiant, but I know better than to grab the camera now and take a picture. She would freak for sure. I answer in English. "It's on the nightstand on your left."

She looks at me like I have grown two heads, so I walk over and pick it up then hand it to her. Finally, she focuses, then smiles a lazy, satisfied smile up at me. "Grazie, Mister Big Man. What time is it?"

When I tell her, I stand back and get out of the storm's path. She blinks rapidly as she absorbs this news and logs it mentally into her calendar, then her eyes widen and a look of sheer panic spreads across her face. She flings the covers off, begins rattling off in Italian how she is late for a gig, then sprints to the foyer where her clothes are. As she dresses, she calls her agent back and leaves a message. "I'm on my way. Do NOT replace me. Ciao."

I stroll in as she is putting on her coat and pulling her hair out. She stops, eyeing my nakedness, and smiles, then bounces up to me and puckers her lips.

"I have to hurry, Americano, but thank you for that fucking of a lifetime." She giggles as I place my lips on her waiting ones. "Let me give you my digits. We can hookup again, no?"

I'm silent. The moment of straight line truth is here. It won't do any good or ease the pain if I tell her she was an exceptional fuck and truly fun, so I just shoot her down. "No."

"No?" She stops, blinks rapidly, then backs up with a confused look on her hurried face.

"That's correct. There are no repeats."

"Ugh!" She yells. The shock of being dumped added to her panic of being late sends her out the studio door. She takes the time to slam it with force before she rushes down the stairs, cussing the entire way. I stroll out to the balcony to watch her run to her car. She stops on the sidewalk, looks up, shakes her fist at me, and screams one more perfect English parting shot. "You're an asshole!"

"Yeah. I am. Ciao." I tell the sports car as it peels off. "Well, that went better than usual," I tell the empty studio as I walk back in. Picking up my camera, I take the digital card from it and mark it #633, then walk through the bedroom to my editing island and put it in the hard drive to upload.

CHAPTER EIGHT

Walking back to the bed, I flop down on it, pull the pillows under my head and grab my phone. I call Darren.

"Aurei! Hey, Bro. What's happening?"

"Ah. Not a whole helluva lot. What's up with you?"

"An investment opportunity has come calling."

"Give me the pitch."

"A few years back I was talking to a Frat brother who owns Been Jammin' in Vegas. He told me he had discovered a dancer who had an unusual idea that turned out to be a gold mine. He called her his million-dollar baby and that she was a bonafide superstar. I told him if he came across another opportunity like that one to give me a call." He pauses. "He called yesterday."

"I'm listening," I tell him.

"This same dancer has been offering a niche service for a select few, very exclusive clientele for years and she has some serious repeat offenders. She came to him with the idea of expansion a few months ago because it's growing faster than she can keep up with and maintain her other obligations." He pauses again.

"I'm listening. What is it?"

"She calls it 'Fucking Fantasies.'" He pauses for effect.

I nod my head at the boldness of the title. "Wow. That's straight line. I'm all ears now."

Darren chuckles. "Bart said anything this girl does makes money. She's like a money magnet and a business guru all rolled into one. He says she is really intelligent and has an intuitiveness that's impressive, but he didn't go into the nitty-gritty of what she actually offers in this niche service. He's keeping that under lock and key for now. Since you're familiar with Vegas, I thought you might be interested, and have some insight or at the least ask you to find out more for me. Do a little digging. I'm definitely interested."

"Sure. I'll check her out for you. What's her name?"

"Seary. Have you heard of her?"

"Hmm. Can't say that I have, but I don't run in those circles. I know people who do though. I can check her out for you. What's the deal your buddy, Bart, is putting together?" I put my feet on the floor and my elbows on my knees and listen to the offer as he discusses the details of the deal. "Sounds like the investment is solid. When do you need an answer on the dancer?"

"Right away. He's gathering the initial capital investors now."

"Ok. I'm actually on Thanksgiving leave at the moment. I'll fly out and evaluate her. I need to touch base on my properties anyway. Do you want me to check in with Bart while I'm there?"

"No. Just spy on her and give me your honest opinion, if you think she's a winner or not, and if you're in or not. I know the deal is a good one."

"Affirmative. I'll let you know by the end of the week."

"Appreciate it."

"No problem. Ciao."

I hang up the phone and immediately begin texting my team.

Antonio: *Change of plans. Charter a plane to Vegas as soon as possible.*

Mia: *I won't be coming by the office after all. Forward the contracts. I'll review and return them from here. Have you heard anything on the issue in North Dakota? Make sure we don't lose that bid. Also, I want to review the list of charities this year and the dollars allocated for each.*

Adona: *Cancel the remainder of the girls. I'm good for now.*

Kip: *I'll be flying in to Vegas in the morning. What are the chances you can get us a couple of tickets into Been Jammin'?*

Maria: *I'll be flying in tomorrow. Would sure appreciate it if I discovered some leftovers waiting for me in the refrigerator.*

Adona responds first. *Is everything good?*

Yes. Leaving Rome. No complaints. She was fun.

Good. I thought you would like her. She is still new to the business. A fresh face. Let me know when you need my services again. You know you are one of my special clients.

Then Kip. *Text me when you're an hour out. I'll pick you up from the airport. Made reservations at the club. Looking forward to the show! Watching strippers dance never gets old.*

Then Antonio: *You'll be flying JetAir. Leaving in two hours.*

I update Angelo: *I'm flying out in two hours. Please pick me up at my apartment in 30.*

Angelo answers: *Roger that, Boss. On my way now.*

Maria sends: *Can't wait to see you! It's been too long. I'll have your favorite waiting. Safe travels."

And last Mia answers. Her text is a chapter in a book, so I flip through it. Scanning it for anything that must be handled now. Nothing that can't wait until I'm in the air.

I head to the bathroom to shave then shower. Lathering up, I stroke my face with the razor, and think about the concept of a Fucking Fantasy business in Vegas where prostitution is legal. All the ideas that come to mind make me realize how uniquely qualified I am to evaluate this particular business venture. Hasn't that been what I've been doing? Having different kinds of sex with different women, experimenting and enjoying all they have to offer? I smile at myself in the mirror. I'm looking forward to learning more about this Fucking Fantasy business. I turn the shower on and step in. Sticking my head under the hot water, I close my eyes and think about nothing. Letting the wet warmth clear my mind and regenerate my body. When I step out, I get dressed in a pair of comfy gym pants and long sleeve t-shirt, then pack, throw on a hoody and leave the apartment. Angelo is already waiting on the street for me. On the way to the airport, we discuss the soccer match.

At the airport, the traffic is heavy, so I tell Angelo. "Pop the trunk. I'll walk in." He gives me a look that says he would rather I not, but does what I say. I grab my bag, and trot to the private terminal, check in and board the plane without incident. Once on board, I pull out my laptop and begin reviewing the documents Mia sent over. Halfway across the Atlantic, I finally finish, sign them and hit send. Then I look over the bid for the North Dakota fracking contract, verify the numbers are where they need to be and give her the go-ahead to negotiate the terms. Next, I review the list of charities and notice that Wounded Warriors isn't on the list. I send her a note to add them and also remind her to make sure she sets up the scholarship for Bradford's children and pays off their home mortgage for his widow. I close the laptop, take the pillow the flight attendant offers and settle in to catch up on my sleep. "Please wake me when we are Stateside. I'd like to eat while the jet refuels."

"Yes, sir. Sleep well." He tells me as he pulls the shutters over the windows, blocking out the sun.

I'm asleep before he finishes.

CHAPTER NINE

....

....

....

I'm driving to the flight line. Bradford sits next to me. Everett's in the back. Bradford is talking about his wife and kids. His youngest just started the first grade. Proud papa. He kisses his school picture and tucks it back inside his flight suit.

Everett unbuckles leans up and shows off a picture too.

Crack! Boom! The vehicle rocks and nearly flips, then lands hard upright, shaking us as it bounces to a stop.

My ears are ringing from the blast. All I can hear is the pounding of my heart in them, drowning everything else out. The world seems to be in slow motion. I survey the cab.

There's blood everywhere.

Bradford hangs dead in the passenger seat.

Anger floods my mind.

Rage drenches my body mixing with the sweat.

Then ... a scream that deafened sanity.

The world speeds back up and the noise is deafening. Everett is screaming.

I yell over it, and command calm, then try to move to help. My harness is locked. The mechanism is jammed. I'm strapped to the seat. I try to rip it, but it's too strong.

My knife is in the leg side pocket of my flight suit. Wedging my leg in the space between the seat and the console, I stretch my arm down to the zipper. My fingers touch the edge of the metal and nimbly I gather the fabric, pushing the zipper open. I continue gathering more fabric with my fingers until I feel the cold metal of my revolver. I flip the snap and pull it from its holster. Quickly cock it, then return it and hunt my buck knife. By the time I pull it from its sheath, there is complete silence. Only the deep, even breathing of Everett fills my ears. I glance back and receive an affirmative nod. I cut the strap and free myself. Lay my fingers on Bradford's neck. His jugular is quiet, confirming his death.

Exiting the vehicle, I quickly survey the danger. Looking around the empty area, I spot a burka running with what looks like an AK47. I move around the vehicle, assessing the damage while I hurry to Everett's aid.

The roadside bomb was a singular hit.

We are immobile.

Trapped.

Stranded.

Alone.

I snatch hard on the damaged door and open it. Only the sound of heavy panting greets me as Everett, who is a seasoned soldier, controls the pain with deep measured intakes and exhales of breath, forcing control, knowing we must contain the situation if we are to get out of this alive.

"Bradford?"

"Dead."

"Fuck!"

I look down to find a badly mangled leg. Blood has saturated the flight suit. I can't tell if it's an artery or a vein. I talk softly while I take my knife and cut the fabric off. "It's pretty bad, Easy, but it's only a flesh wound. You'll live, but you can't move it." Our eyes briefly connect as I unzip my flight suit, and pull my arms out, letting it hang off my ass as I pull my t-shirt off. Both of us know that means target. I make a command decision. "Call it in and lay low. I'm going after the motherfucker. Shoot anyone who isn't wearing an American uniform. That's an order."

Everett nods.

I tie my t-shirt above the wound and cinch it tight, knowing the pressure is lifesaving. "Tourniquet. Just in case." I try to offer reassurance.

"Dead."

"Fuck!"

I look down to find a badly mangled leg. Blood has saturated the flight suit. I can't tell if it's an artery or a vein. I talk softly while I take my knife and cut the fabric off. "It's pretty bad, Easy, but it's only a flesh wound. You'll live, but you can't move it." Our eyes briefly connect as I unzip my flight suit, and pull my arms out, letting it hang off my ass as I pull my t-shirt off. Both of us know that means target. I make a command decision. "Call it in and lay low. I'm going after the motherfucker. Shoot anyone who isn't wearing an American uniform. That's an order."

Everett nods.

I tie my t-shirt above the wound and cinch it tight, knowing the pressure is lifesaving. "Tourniquet. Just in case." *I try to offer reassurance.*

"I know. Go."

I turn toward the closest building as I pull my flight suit back on, estimate the time that has ticked off, the distance to it, the time it will take me to run there, and whether the motherfucker is hiding inside. As I reach into my pocket to retrieve my weapon, I hear Everett say in a voice just above a whisper. "Hard, my gun is jammed."

Without hesitation, I hand mine over. "Here. Take mine. That's also an order."

I reach back in for my buck knife. As my fingers wrap around the handle, a feeling of calmness fills me. 'Hand to hand it will be then.' *I pull it from its sheath, knowing all the years of training will give me the advantage. I see Augustus as I sprint to the building and hear the pride in his voice when he named me, The Bastard Son of Thor.*

Entering the doorway, I slide quietly in. Checking the space for movement. Listening with the intensity of a hunter. Knowing my prey is close, but not knowing if the enemy is a lone wolf or a member of a pack. Every sense on high alert, I move from room to room. No one.

Climbing the steps to the first floor, I hear muffled voices coming from the room at the top. When I push open the bedroom door, a shocking sight awaits. Two women huddle together in the middle of the floor with one, two ... six small children lying face down. Their tiny faces hidden. Tiny hands over their ears. Only their sniffles can be heard. Along the wall to my right are three preteen boys standing at attention, but shaking with eyes bulging. Their faces full of fear.

'Only a coward would hide here.'

"Shush." I raise my finger to my lips and begin to back away, pulling the door closed, watching the eyes of the young boys. As they lose focus on me and see what's behind the door, sheer terror fills their faces, then an automatic weapon begins spraying bullets. The women scream and fall over the children whose cries are more like wails. The young boys' bodies fall to the floor and blood stains the wall behind them.

I kick the door open, driving it into the wall and thunder into the room with the ferocity of the roman heritage that pumps through my veins. Hell bent on securing not only Easy's safety and the safety of the innocents but having my revenge for Bradford's death. I charge the enemy as the gun sprays the room. He tries to control it and turn it on me, but I reach him first. My left-hand smashes into his throat while my right stabs the knife to the hilt directly in the ball of his shoulder. The gun drops to his side and sprays rounds into the floor. I drive my body into his with crushing power and yank the knife out. My choke hold pinches off the scream of pain and I lift the enemy combatant off the floor, feeling like a raging bear, needing to look him in the eye. Blood soaks the burka deep red and the sight is satisfying.

I stare ruthlessly at the red face of the murdering coward and see not a man, but a demon staring back. I can feel his jugular pounding to be free and remember the feeling of Bradford's lifeless one. Laying the edge of my sharp blade against it, I slowly drag it across, using the edge of my thumb as a guide as my eyes pierce his evil eyes. As the blade slips through his skin, I watch them turn into the fearful eyes of a mortal man who knows death has arrived to claim him. I whisper his death name to him. "Motherfucker!" Then I slice his lifeline.

Blood bursts forth with a velocity that shoots the ceiling, spraying it, painting it dark red.

Silence falls heavy, filling the room with a deafening sound. I hold my attack until there is no life left, then I nimbly flip the knife through my fingers and return it to its sheath in my pocket. Its job is done. As I release the murdering enemy combatant, I take the automatic weapon from his lifeless grip as the dead weight hits the floor with an echoing thud. I turn the gun on the innocent occupants, no one is moving. Silent eyes stare at me.

My cold eyes stares back.

Hard-Core.

The only sound I hear is of my own blood thumping and my own calm breath inhaling and exhaling in rhythm with it. When the soldiers burst into the room, I watch the scene unfold as if in slow motion again. They stand guard over the women and children, search the dead teen boys, give the all clear signal and escort the survivors from the room. As they pass, the little ones' eyes pierce me to my core. The pain, the fear, the unknown. When the women pass, their eyes are turned down as they approach, but one cuts hers at me and I see hopelessness.

Everett!

Rushing back down the stairs, real-time returns and my hand finds its way to my own jugular. The pounding comforts me. I stop in the doorway just long enough to assess the current conditions outside and wipe the blood from my hands before I enter the light. Soldiers are everywhere, combing the area for more IEDs; and more enemy combatants. The situation is under control.

I step into the light and the intensity of the warmth feels good. I'm alive. Making my way back to the vehicle, I arrive just as a medic exits. Looking in, I breathe a sigh of relief. My crew chief sits there smiling.

"You good, Easy?"

"Always," Everett says with a smirk and heavily glazed eyes. "Morphine is my new best friend." I chuckle at that truth. "Did you take care of business?"

"Always," I reply with the same smirk.

"Smart ass!" Then Everett's eyes clear and they look directly into mine. "Did you find the motherfucker?"

"Affirmative."

"Dead?"

"Yeah."

"Good!" She looks down at her mangled leg, then at the front seat where Bradford sat.

"Bradford?"

"He's been escorted back."

"Good." We stare at each other, knowing the pain of his death will bond us together forever. She opens her mouth to ask. I know she wants the details so I begin telling her before she has too. "The Motherfucker was hiding as a woman."

"Piece of shit!" The venom in her voice is pure.

"Yeah. Hiding with the women and children."

"Are they okay?"

"He killed three boys before I could get my hands on him."

She looks up. "Are you good?"

"Yeah." I smile at her, raise my arms and turn around so she can see, I'm unscathed. "I'm good."

"How did you...."

"Knife," I answer before she can classify the killing, then hold my hand out. "My gun, please, Ma'am."

She stares at my open hand, digesting the information,

and realizing I'm not going to share any more details. She quietly lays the weapon in it. I check the safety then return it to its holster and zip it up with the buck knife. "Looks like you'll be heading home now."

She looks down at her leg. "Yeah. Looks like a one-way ticket out of here." She takes a deep breath, then relaxes, letting the morphine have its way with her. When she looks up at me again, she says. "Easy Mama's going home to see my Badass Baby Daddy!"

The look on her face makes my breath hang in my throat and my gut tighten. Wow!

She closes her eyes and drifts off to sleep and I stand there guarding her. When the medics return with a gurney, I wake her. "Easy. Time to go home." Her eyes flutter and when she focuses on me, she smiles.

I continue standing guard over my friend as they remove her. When she passes me, she raises up on one arm and holds her hand out. I walk over to clasp it.

"Take care of yourself, Easy. Your Badass Baby Daddy is one lucky man."

"Will do, Sir. You too." She grins, then laughs, falling back onto the gurney. "Yes, he is!" I watch for just a moment, then walk away, knowing it's time to report to my commanding officer.

FINDING HER

I hear her yell after me. "Hey, Hard? Don't stay that way."

I throw my hand up in the air, letting her know I heard her.

"I'm serious, Asshole!" She yells.

That makes me laugh out loud, so I turn to face her but continue walking backwards. "It's who I am." I grin and double tap my heart with a closed fist. "Hard-Core." Then I spin around and continue walking away.

She laughs and yells again. "Don't forget hard head."

I sling both arms in the air, spin to face her again and give her a final salute, flipping her off. "Affirmative, it's a steel trap too. I won't forget you, Easy Mama."

"You better not!"

"I won't."

I can't.

....

....

....

CHAPTER TEN

The shutters in the cabin are lifted one by one and the brightness brings me back to reality. I hear the flight attendant step up beside me and I acknowledge I'm awake by lifting my hand, but I keep my eyes closed, wanting to stay in that moment for as long as possible before consciousness arrives and the memory blurs. As the vision that haunts me vanishes out of sight, my gut tightens and I wonder.... Easy's face. Full of undeniable love. It was unadulterated beauty. Will I ever have someone who looks at me that way?

The plane touches down. Fully awake now, I brace myself for the momentum of the brakes. When the plane taxis down the runway, I pinch the bridge of my nose and let the raw emotions that the dream left settle back down. Leaning my head back, pushing them down deep inside, not forgotten, but not harbored, I gain control. They are a part of who I am now. I take a deep cleansing breath. War fucking sucks balls, but Warriors win.

I unbuckle and visit the restroom. When I return, my food has been served. The flight attendant stands by the seat, smiling at me. "Mr. Moore, what would you like to drink? Coffee? Water? Or perhaps something else? We have Crown Royal in the freezer."

That makes me smile. It's always nice when your preferred drink of choice is remembered. "I'm good with water. Thank you."

I spend the remainder of the flight to Vegas going over the architect's plans for the farmhouse in Alabama and making notes on the changes I want. About an hour out, I text Kip to let him know. When the plane touches down, I'm caught up and ready to move forward.

Walking down the steps, I see Kip. He throws his hand up and I wave back.

When I arrive at his car, he shakes my hand and slaps my back in a bro hug. "Aurei, it's good to see you, brother." He takes my bag and throws it in the trunk.

"Likewise, buddy."

Kip is not only my real estate agent, but he's a close friend. When I first began investing in the real estate market in Vegas, he was a fireman dabbling in real estate remodeling on his off days. Kip showed me his first 'fixer-upper' and I negotiated with him to do the work. Since then, he manages my portfolio, buying and flipping fixer-uppers, while his wife manages my rental units.

"Bianca sends her love."

"How's she doing?"

"Ornery as ever." Kip smiles.

"That's why you're still together. She don't take shit off you."

Kip laughs. "True dat. She's one tough little bitch."

I laugh. "Does she know you call her that?"

"Hell no! And don't you go telling her either." He changes the subject. "So, do you want to do the house tour now, or do you want to go to your place first and rest. We'll head to Been Jammin' around midnight. If Surreal is performing, we don't want to miss her."

"I'm up for a tour now. I slept on the plane, but I want to be back to the house to see the sunset. I'll meet you at Been Jammin'."

"Good deal. Let's start with the latest purchases and we'll work our way down the list." Kip gives me the rundown as he drives. "This last batch of remodels are almost ready to flip. I think this team of subs is doing a better job than the last one. I have a group of fifteen houses I'm putting together to show to some Japanese investors." We spend the afternoon looking at properties, crisscrossing blocks and suburbs.

When we've seen the last one, I ask him as he drives me back to my place. "Have you gone to Been Jammin' before?"

"Yeah. It's a happening place. Have you been yet?"

"No, I haven't. Tell me what you know about it."

"It's the hottest gentlemen's club in Vegas. I had to call in some favors to get us in tonight."

"Thanks for that. I appreciate it."

"Are you hoping to catch a Surreal Show? 'Cause they don't announce them ahead of time."

"No. I was wondering if you are familiar with the dancers?"

He cuts his eyes at me and his eyebrows are raised. His voice is cautiously curious. "Somewhat. I'm not the regular I used to be since I hooked up with Bianca.

She's coming tonight, by the way. She insisted." He laughs and mimics her voice, making me laugh. "'You'll be horny as hell within an hour and no one's riding that hose but me.' But I know it's really to see you."

I crack up at that, knowing it's true and thankful it's open between us. Kip and Bianca are into BDSM and belong to a private club. She has been determined to get me to join them for a threesome for a long time now, but I ain't into that.

He chuckles. "She won't stop you know."

I laugh. "I know, but it ain't happening."

He laughs now too. "I keep telling her that if you haven't already caved in to her, you aren't going to, but she is a pitbull at heart."

I shake my head.

He goes back to my question. "Why do you ask about the dancers at Been Jammin'? Have you been referred to one?"

"Yes. Her name is Seary."

Kip whistles. "Damn man. Nothing like shooting for the Star. Seary's the headliner there."

"Tell me everything you know about her."

FINDING HER

"She's as hot as her name implies."

I wait, but he doesn't offer any more information. "That's all you know?"

"Well. Yeah. She's the Star. I don't have the pocketbook to know more than that."

I nod and look out the window, then after a few moments, I ask. "How much does she cost?"

Kip hits the brakes and slows down to a stop at the red light before he answers. He turns in the seat and looks me in the eye. "You're looking to score with her?"

"Maybe."

He grins, then takes off again. "I wish you luck, bro. I've never heard anyone talk about hitting that ho, but I know they do book her." He hits the blinker and pulls up to my house. "Are you sure you don't want to ride with us?"

"I'm sure. I'll meet you at the club."

"Ask for Beverly."

"Will do. Thanks for the tour. You're doing a great job."

He grins, gives me a head nod and I walk around to the trunk to retrieve my bag. I hoist it out, then slam the trunk, double tap it and he pulls away."

CHAPTER ELEVEN

Walking up to my 4,000 plus square foot, 4 bedroom, 4 bath luxury house in the Red Rock Country Club Community in Summerlin, I wonder again why I bought such a big house when there is only me to live in it and part-time at that. I lay my thumb on the keypad at the security gate, then again at the front door and enter the quiet house. Dropping the bag on the marble floor, my footsteps sound as I walk straight out to the backyard to enjoy the magnificent view of the Red Rock sunset. Standing there watching the ball of fire dropping in the sky, I remember why I bought this big house. It has the most spectacular, breathtaking view of the setting sun and I'm grateful again for my good fortune.

The motion sensor exterior security lights illuminate the green carpet of grass as I turn to go back to the house. The pool water has turned green and provides a soft glow on the patio area. I strip, toss my clothes on a bench, take a deep breath, and dive in. Swimming underwater to the opposite side, I enjoy the peaceful silence and the warmth is soothing. Surfacing, I fill my lungs full, toss my head to the side out of habit from my long hair days as a kid, and blow the water running down my face off my lips.

Knowing I have plenty of time, I dive back under the water, but surface to swim on top, letting my hands cut it like a knife as they enter, pulling my muscular frame, gliding effortlessly along, kicking only to keep my balance. At the end, I do a flip and push off to continue swimming nonstop. I end up swimming thirty complete laps, which is almost a half mile and I feel great. Putting my hands on the pool's edge, I push up out of the water, throw my foot up and stand in the cold air. Goosebumps pop out and I shake like a dog to expel the water, then grab my clothes off the bench and hurry back into the warmth of the house. Racing nothing but my cold nakedness, I run to the foyer to get my bag, tuck it under my arm like a football player, and sprint to the laundry room. The automatic motion sensors turn the lights on in each room as I go and turn them off as I leave. I drop my bag in front of the washing machine and find a towel folded neatly on top along with a pair of gym shorts and a note from Maria, my house sitter.

"Aurelius, I know you didn't grab a towel from the pool house after your swim. It's too cold to be running around soaking wet and put these shorts on. It's also too cold to be running around naked." I smirk. She knows me too well. "Leftovers are in the refrigerator as requested. Let's do breakfast tomorrow and catch up. Text me when you wake and I'll come up to start cooking. Oh! And do NOT start laundry. I'll do it tomorrow. I mean it! Don't!" I laugh at that and kick the bag to the wall out of the way, dry off with the towel, drape it over my shoulders, don the gym shorts and head to the weight room.

As soon as I enter, I raise my arms in the air and announce to the emptiness. "Pumping iron is good for the raging beast that lives within us." I work my way around the machines and finish in about 40 minutes. When I walk out, my muscles feel swollen and I feel like I can handle anything that comes my way.

Heading into the kitchen, I open the fridge and stick my face inside. Umm. Homemade enchiladas! I mix an after-workout protein shake and take it with me up the stairs to shower. Stepping under the water, I lather and think about my goal for tonight. I simply want to see her dance. If I like what I see, I'll book her and find out firsthand what her deal is.

I hear Kip's voice again. She's as hot as her name implies. You're looking to score with her? If she comes up with a Fucking Fantasy that impresses me, I might let her work some magic on me. I haven't fucked anyone outside my studio in Rome for years. Hell, if she comes up with one I haven't thought of, I might invest myself.

But then I hear Kip again as he so poetically put it. I've never heard anyone talk about hitting that ho. Why is that? Kip has eyes and ears all over Vegas. Someone should've talked about popping that pussy. The thought that Bart could be scamming his Frat buddy makes me determined to check her out. Darren's a good guy.

Turning the water off, I step out and decide to skip shaving. I'm on leave. No need to be smooth shaven, but I splash Old Spice after shave on anyway, squirt some mousse in my hair and run my fingers through it to stand my thick blonde hair up. Then I go into the dressing room to choose my clothes for the evening. Pressing the button, the closet doors slide inside the wall until my entire wardrobe is on display. I walk in and pick a dark purple J Crew shirt and dark jeans. I'll blend in with the shadows and have a better opportunity to watch this dancer work.

Walking back out, I push the button again, and the doors slide closed. Then I push the button below it, and the cabinet doors of the opposite wall slide back and my shoes rise in a stair step display case. I grab the black Converse tennis shoes, hit the button on my way out to close the cabinet and go into the bedroom to actually get dressed. Stepping into my jeans, I am thankful for Albert, my tailor, who customizes my jeans. The soft, distressed, fabric sits snug on my thighs and hugs my ass, but there is plenty of room in the crotch for my balls to dangle. Putting my arms in the shirt sleeves, I realize my biceps are tight in the fabric and when I pull the shirt closed to button it, I feel it hug tight across my back. Hmm. Note to self. Call Albert. I need to be measured again. I've gained more muscle mass. I leave the first four buttons undone to accommodate my new size.

Opening the safe, I take enough cash to have a good time at the gaming tables if Seary is a dud and an open limit credit card in case I lose my ass gambling early on. I have no intentions of coming back to a lonely house before the sun rises. I fold the money around the credit card and slide the wad into a money clip, then put it in my front pocket. Slipping into my shoes, I glance at my reflection in the mirror as I stand and I hear "Mister Very Big Man with the very big ass" making me chuckle. True dat.

Trotting down the stairs, I head to the kitchen to heat Maria's famous enchiladas. While I eat, I catch up on the news, then wash my dishes. Walking across the house to the garage, my mood is light and carefree. I think I'll drive the Corvette. Sliding behind the wheel, I check the settings and the mirrors, then back out, and drive down to the security gate.

Waiting for it to open, I tune the cars sound system to my playlist and turn it up. The speakers are booming with the bass. Once I'm out on the open road, I push its limits. The car screams down the interstate. I love flying. An hour later, I'm heading back to Vegas and decide to visit Fremont Street.

CHAPTER TWELVE

It's alive with lights, music, sounds and people milling around. Stopping at a red light, I see an Elvis street performer having his picture taken with a tourist, some young girls with only body paint and g-strings on, and two nuns wearing habits that have their enormous, naked tits hanging out. I circle around and at the next red light, I'm enjoying a Michael Jackson impersonator, who is really good, when I hear a TAP, TAP, TAP. I look out the passenger window and see a young girl smiling at me with her tits about to fall out of her dress. I roll the window down and she asks me. "Are you our Uber?"

Really? I'm in a Corvette. It's a two seater! I laugh out loud and tell her. "No." But she has stood up and is talking to her friend and doesn't hear me. Her hand is resting on the door in the open window. I lean over so she can hear me. She is giggling with her friend and I realize they are very drunk. I also realize Vegas is not without predators and she is putting them in danger standing on the corner of Fremont Street asking strangers for lifts. I make a command decision, reach over and pop the door open. Without hesitation, the giggling girl pulls it open and plops down in the passenger seat. The interior lights come on and I see 6-inch-high stiletto heels enter the car first, then big thighs, followed by a miniskirt stretch taut like a tent. Her sweater top has a scoop neck and she has it pulled down too low. She doesn't look at me, but rather prepares to receive her skinny friend. The tiny girl plops down in her lap, tucks her knees up under her chin, then turns back and attempts to close the door.

Their giggles fill the small space.

The traffic light turns green.

The car behind us honks.

The door doesn't shut.

I lean back over and stick my arm between them. "Here. Let me get that for you." When my hand moves theirs aside and grasps the door handle, both of them stop moving and quit giggling. They watch as I pull the door firmly shut then turn to look at me. I smile and ask. "Where to ladies?"

The curvy one's jaw literally falls open and the skinny one's eyes nearly bug out of her thin face, the light dims and they burst into mad giggling again. I check the mirrors and the pedestrians before I pull out, while they whisper.

"Holy fucking hell! What a hottie!"

"His eyes. Did you see his eyes?"

Tapping the gas, I ease away and ask again. "Where to ladies?" I glance over to see they are both staring at me and it makes me laugh.

Then the curvy girl answers. "Excalibur."

"Cool." I introduce myself, offering my hand. "Hi. I'm Aurei Moore."

The skinny girl takes it. "Hi. I'm Stella." She turns a pretty shade of pink and I can tell right away that Stella in not as drunk as I first thought, but very shy.

"Hi. I'm Nina." The girl on bottom introduces herself and pokes Stella, who lets my hand drop.

I return it to the steering wheel and give them a wink.

"Are you ladies, here for a wedding or celebrating graduation?"

Stella pushes her glasses up her nose. "Graduation."

Graduation? I cut my eyes at them again. Are they 22? They look a lot younger. Surely they are college graduates and not high school. "Where did you go to college?"

"USC." Nina offers without missing a beat. Damn. They must be 22. I look over again, sizing them up and feel ... old. Must be my tours of duty.

"First time to Vegas?"

"Yeah!"

"First day?"

"Yeah!" They giggle again.

"What are you girls going to see at the Excalibur? The Tournament of Kings?"

They laugh and high-five each other. "No. The Thunder From Down Under."

"Of course," I smirk. Where else would two young girls needing to blow off steam on their first night in Vegas want to go?

Stella leans down to hear what Nina whispers and she answers. "Right? That would be fucking fly!"

I can feel their eyes staring at me. Gawking actually. I reach over to adjust the temperature. "Is it warm enough for you?"

Stella says. "Oh yes. I'm really warm."

"I'm getting down right hot in here," Nina says, then bursts into a new round of drunken giggles and Stella can't help but join her. It's infectious and I chuckle too.

As soon as it gets quiet, they resume their gawking again and it's awkward. I keep my eyes on the road and try to keep the conversation from going any further south. "What did you major in?"

Nina answers. "I majored in education."

"A teacher, then."

"I bet I could teach you a thing or too." She says under her breath.

I ask Stella. "And you? Are you a teacher too?"

Nina snorts and I look at them. "No, she majored in...."

Stella cuts her eyes at Nina, shooting darts, and fills in the answer. "Security. I majored in security."

I can't hide my surprise with that answer. This girl weighs all of 100 pounds. "Security? Really? You don't look like a badass."

A smirk plays on her lips. She is trying hard not to join her giggling friend. "It's I.T. security."

"Are you a hacker?" I look back at the road.

Nina snorts again. "Sort of. It's in social engineering." I cut my eyes at them. Now they have my attention.

"Social engineering? What's that?" I play dumb.

Stella looks out the window and answers with a straight face. "I find and prevent perps from screwing corporate accounts up." She doesn't take her eye off the sights outside.

"Hmm. I've heard they can infiltrate and hold servers hostage. Is that true?"

She looks surprised at me. "Yes. Absolutely and some of the really bad dudes have even demanded ransoms!"

"How do you find these bad guys?"

Nina burst out laughing again and we both look at her. "She performs penetration tests. HAHAHAHA!"

I can't help but laugh with her and Stella smiles when I ask. "Really? What kind of penetration tests?"

She clears her throat and tries valiantly to be professional. "I'm a white hat."

Nina can't help herself. She leans on the door and cackles, making me chuckle with her again.

Stella manages to remain serious. "Do you know what that is?"

"I do." I smile and wink.

Nina comes up for air and blurts. "My best friend is a virtual corporate condom." Then she snorts again and gives in to the giggles.

Stella laughs with us and tells me. "Wait for it. She's not finished."

"She's going to be going down on all the big dickheads too. HAHAHAHA! That's sooooo fuuuuucking fuuuuuunny!"

We enjoy a good laugh as I maneuver to the curb outside Excalibur. "We have arrived, Ladies." Nina starts wiping her eyes and getting her giggles under control.

"The men from the Outback await you. I hope you enjoyed your ride." I lean over and pop the door open for them. Stella twists in the tight space, holds her phone up and asks. "Mind if we snapchat?"

I grin. "I don't mind."

They do their thing, I give them a thumbs-up and a nice smile, then Stella gets out. Nina twists, puts her feet on the sidewalk and tries to rise. "Oh fuck! I'm stuck." She bursts out laughing again. "Stell, give me a hand."

She does and Nina grasps it and does her best to lift her ass up while Stella leans back, pulling as hard as she can, but it's not enough. Nina is stuck. She lets go of Stella's hand and plops back on the seat, while Stella stumbles backward, trying not to fall. Nina has another fit of giggles and I know she won't be able to get out as long as she's laughing, so I lean over, put my mouth right next to her ear, and drop my voice to a very deep tone, giving her a taste of seduction. "Baby Girl. You're gonna need some big strong hands to help." Her laughter dies immediately. She freezes, listening. My voice stays low. "The problem with 6" heels in a sports car that's only 15" off the road is the center of gravity shifts." She turns her head and looks me in the eye. I can smell the liquor on her breath. "I can help you if you want."

"What do you suggest?" Her voice is breathless.

"You can take your shoes off and climb out on your own, or I can give you a push."

"What kind of push?" She smirks, flirting.

"The kind that you will remember for the rest of your life."

She grins and says. "I'm down for that."

I grin back. "Good Girl. Lean up as far as you can."

She does as instructed. I place my hands on her waist, rubbing her with my thumbs to relax her. I then slide my fingertips down her curves, forcing them between her miniskirt and the leather of the car seat. Cupping her ass and squeezing her as I go, I inch my fingers down towards her pussy. When they leave the miniskirt behind and touch her bare skin, she says in a voice that shows she is thrilled she chose this method. "Oh my!"

"You're so hot!" I whisper in her ear as they inch further under her into heaving position. When her ass is sitting on my hands and part of my forearms, I ask. "Ready, Baby?"

"Yes." Her voice is full of anticipation.

"Ok. Here's what I want you to do for me." I whisper in her ear. I see Stella's shoes come into view, but Nina waves her away. "On the count of three, I'm going to thrust my hands up and I want you to enjoy it, arching your back, and pushing those beautiful tits of yours up to the stars."

"Oh, my!" She says again.

"Can you do that?"

"Yes." She takes a deep breath. "I can do that."

"Ok. Here we go." I lay my lips on her ear and breathe into it, then I whisper. "One.

Two." I blow in it while I grip her ass firmly, curling my fingertips into her skin.

"Oh. Fuck!" She says, with a voice that tells me my fingers are pulling her pussy open.

"Three," I tell her with a commanding voice, while I heave her ass up. She arches her back, pushes her tits to the stars and her ass lifts out of the seat, as I push her from the car. For a moment, she rocks on her heels, then staggers forward a little until she gains control of the momentum, then she burst into a fit of giggles again and jumps up and down, asking Stella. "Did you get that? Did you get it? Please! For fucks sake! Tell me you got it."

Stella holds up the phone and says. "I did! I did! Calm down. You're gonna break your heels." Nina snatches the phone from her friend and begins to watch the replay, while

Stella sticks her head in the car. Pushing her glasses up, she tells me. "We appreciate the ride."

"You betcha." I reach for a business card. "You do realize I'm not an Uber right?"

She grins. "Yeah. It was a dare."

"Ah!" I laugh and hand my card to her.

She takes it, reads it, then smiles. "Maximus Enterprises, huh?"

I nod. "When you get home, look me up. I could use your skills."

Her smile is radiant. "I will. Thanks." Then she closes the door. I check the traffic, then I hear TAP, TAP, TAP. I put the window down.

Nina sticks her head inside, grinning from ear to ear. "Thanks for the lift."

"No problem." I give her a wink.

"I'll never forget it."

I grin, knowing she won't. "You ladies enjoy the Thunder From Down Under show."

"You dancing tonight?" Her giggles return.

I chuckle and shake my head. "No."

"Too bad. I was going to return the favor." She curls her fingers in a claw and I laugh out loud. Then she makes a fist and shoves it at me. "Hashtag Hottest Uber Ever!"

I give her a knuckle bump. "You girls stay safe."

As I pull away, I hear her tell Stella. "Fucking awesome dare, Stell!"

CHAPTER THIRTEEN

Been Jammin' is down the strip from the Excalibur. When I pull in, I drive under the canopy and wait my turn for valet parking. An older man takes my information, then takes my car. When I enter the building, I notice several things. One, like all the other casinos, there are a lot of people coming and going, but unlike the others, there isn't a hotel associated with it.

When you enter Been Jammin', you step immediately into the casino area and the sounds of the slot machines hit you. They have their own distinct music. Each time I hear it, I know I'm home.

I find the sign that says Gentleman's Club and I head that way, taking my time and enjoy my stroll. Deeper into the casino, I hear "Wheel of Fortune" and the click,

click, click of a simulated wheel turning, then someone squeals. They've hit the jackpot. Passing the gambling tables, I stop and take my time to study the limits and dealers. Walking around the whole area knowing if I'm going to play, I want to find the right fit. I need to find a dealer who is engaging the table. Most of the dealers are stiff and polite, but across the area, I can see a crowd around one so I head that way. When I get close enough, I stop and observe a red head in a tight, black corset with overflowing tits, plump buttocks and a full table of gamblers. She is laughing and as she deals the whole table cheers. People are stopping to watch. She's the one. I'll come back to her table.

Turning away, I locate again the sign that points to the Gentleman's Club. I pass several stores selling merchandise. When I pass the Steakhouse Restaurant, the aroma smells good, and I decide to eat breakfast there.

I take my phone out and text Maria. *Better make our date lunch.*

Okay. :(

I smile at the phone and return it to my pocket. She's the best. Just past the restaurant, there is construction going on, and the path narrows. Walking along it, I notice there aren't any signs on the wall saying what is being built and I wonder if it is to accommodate the Fucking Fantasy expansion.

When the path opens up, I have arrived at the Gentleman's Club. The atmosphere is set with a small patio style area outside the triple set of entrance doors. Cocktail tables with simple straight back chairs are placed inside the railing and waitresses clad in nothing more that pasties and G-strings comb the area serving drinks. It's packed and the sound of conversations buzz over the piped music from inside. At the gate in the railing, there are two hostesses at the podium. I walk over and they greet me with pleasant smiles. "Good evening, Sir. How may we serve you?"

"Good evening, ladies. I'm looking for Beverly."

"She's inside. Is she expecting you?"

"Later in the evening."

"I can text her someone is waiting to see her if you like?"

"Thank you."

"Sure." She takes her phone. "Who may say is here?"

"Aurelius Moore."

Her eyebrows flinch, telling me she wasn't expecting

Aurelius, then she begins texting. The other hostess asks me. "May we offer you a drink while you wait?"

"That would be nice. I'll have Crown neat, please."

She also takes her phone and sends a text.

"Beverly will be right out."

I nod and step back to let another patron approach. While I wait, I examine the banners hanging from the rafters over the area. All of them are advertising a dancer named Surreal, but they appear to be of Brittney Spears, Jennifer Lopez, Katy Perry and other performers. In the center is the only one that has an unknown dancer. She has black and gold hair and her face is covered by a bejeweled Mardi Gras mask. The banner shows her gripping a stripper pole at her pussy and doing a full split on it. Her arms are pushing her big tits out of an open heart-shaped hole. Hmm. Her body is fucking hot! I thought Kip said Seary was the headliner, but this girl is definitely the star attraction.

When I turn back to the hostess podium to ask, I almost knock my drink out of the hands of a nice-looking woman dressed in a red sequined gown. My reflexes catch the drink and stabilize it in her hands. She is unfazed, smiling and introduces herself. "Mr.

Moore, I'm Beverly. Welcome to Been Jammin'. How may I assist you?"

"I'm going to gamble at table #56. I would appreciate a call when my party arrives."

"Certainly. I will see to it personally. Have you enjoyed our tables before?"

"No. I can't say that I have."

"Well, allow me to register you so you won't have to cash out your chips."

"I appreciate that."

"This way." She turns and I follow as she steps around the patio area and enters a black side door with a key code that is next to invisible to the naked, untrained eye. We step into a plush hallway with doors leading off each side. A showgirl enters with an older gentleman in tow. She escorts him into one of the side doors and closes it. Beverly explains. "This area is reserved for our VIP members. I would be happy to schedule you a tour. My office is right here." She opens the door and waves me inside.

I enter to find a large office with a desk at one end, and a couch and two sitting chairs framing a coffee table at the other. There are autographed pictures of her with a who's who of icons in the entertainment industry. The celebrities vary from Wayne Newton to Justin Bieber. I step up to the wall and begin scanning all the pictures. While she walks to her desk, takes the laptop off, and goes to sit on to the couch. "Let's get you hooked up."

I smile at her words, then dig my money clip out of my pocket, unwrap the credit card and hand it to her with a smile.

She smiles back, closes her computer, stands and takes the card, then walks back to her desk while I sit down, and enjoy the drink she brought me. I ask her the questions I have while I watch her scan it, knowing it will answer all her questions.

"Who is Surreal?"

She glances up. "She's our star performer."

"Who is Seary?"

"She's our headliner."

She opens a drawer and takes a card out, and activates it.

"How much are your VIP rooms?"

"That's between you and your choice from our talented dancers." She smiles and hands me both cards. "Present our card whenever you are here in the club. It will be all you need."

I stand and return them in my pants pocket. "Thanks." Bending back down to pick up my unfinished drink, I ask. "What's the difference between being a star and being a headliner? Besides the money."

She laughs as she shows me out the way we came. "One is an entertainer, one is a dancer." I eye the door at the end of the hall, but it is quiet and I realize the rooms are completely sound proof. This must be where Seary gives her Fucking Fantasies.

When she shows me through the hidden side door, I ask. "May I access this door with my card? I'm a very private man."

She shakes her head. "I'm afraid not. All customers must use the nightclub to enter. I'm sure you understand." She pulls the door closed, making sure it is locked, then smiles at me and says. "It was a pleasure meeting you. I'll send you notification when your party arrives." I nod and offer my hand to shake. She takes it and I give her my undivided and unwavering attention, letting my eyes absorb hers. Sometimes a woman needs only the slightest touch to be reminded that they are desirable. I run my thumb lightly over her skin. She inhales a deep breath. "Our staff will take good care of you. If you need my assistance, you need only ask."

"I appreciate your time tonight, Beverly. Thank you."

She tilts her head and nods. "It was my pleasure. Rebecca is working table #56. She'll be expecting you." I give her the same tilting head nod, then walk away. She calls after me. "Good luck. I'll see again at midnight."

I raise my hand, acknowledging I heard her.

CHAPTER FOURTEEN

When I arrive at Rebecca's table, there is still a crowd surrounding it and the same 5 people gambling. Two of them are laughing and three of them are not, but all of them have a nice stack of chips. Rebecca looks up and says to me. "Mr. Moore. It's good to see you."

I grin. "Likewise, Rebecca."

She smiles and deals another round to the table. She asks as she waits for them to give her direction. "Will you be playing with me tonight?"

I chuckle. Was that an innuendo? "Perhaps I will get lucky."

She drops her eyes and grins as she makes her way down the five players with another card. The three who weren't grinning upon my arrival take a hit and bust their hands before she ever shows her card. The first two stayed, and she flips her card to reveal blackjack. Everyone groans and she leans forward to collect their chips, giving everyone an ample view of her cleavage.

When she stands back up, I ask her. "How long are you working tonight?"

"Until dawn." She tells me while she deals another round.

The first two players take a hit and stay at 17. The next two are at 19. Everyone is smiling. The last one takes a hit and wins with 21. Rebecca turns her card over to reveal she has a Queen and a ten. They groan again. The player on the end looks at me and says. "You can have my spot, bro. Her luck is changing."

I sit down and hand her my new Been Jammin' card. She swipes it, then slides it back with a large stack of chips. I can feel the eyes of the others gamblers on us. I peel two off the top and push them back to her. She accepts the tip graciously, then turns her attention back to the entire table and says. "Place your bets."

I put four chips in the betting circle and watch her manicured hands deal the cards. I can tell by the way she handles the deck that she has been a dealer for years. I sit in smiling. The last one takes a hit and wins with 21. Rebecca turns her card over to reveal she has a Queen and a ten. They groan again. The player on the end looks at me and says. "You can have my spot, bro. Her luck is changing."

I sit down and hand her my new Been Jammin' card. She swipes it, then slides it back with a large stack of chips. I can feel the eyes of the others gamblers on us. I peel two off the top and push them back to her. She accepts the tip graciously, then turns her attention back to the entire table and says. "Place your bets."

I put four chips in the betting circle and watch her manicured hands deal the cards. I can tell by the way she handles the deck that she has been a dealer for years. I sit in silence, playing each round and paying attention to the cards as they pass through the deck. I'm not an accomplished card counter, but I'm not unskilled when it comes to blackjack either. As it turns out, I do win more chips than I lose.

After an hour, the original gamblers have all left and before others take their place, I question her.

"How long have you worked here?" I push my chips to place my bet.

"Three years."

"Have you always been a dealer?"

"No. I started off as a dancer." She deals the hand.

"Why aren't you dancing now?"

She smiles. "Better hours and less work."

"Ah!" I fall silent and tap the table to take a hit. She flips a queen up and I bust. I lean back and stretch my arms as she takes my chips, enjoying the view. A cocktail waitress stops next to me and asks if I would like a drink. I order my usual, then ask Rebecca as I bet again.

"So who is Surreal?"

"She's our star attraction."

"Is she any good?"

She smirks at me, raises an eyebrow and repeats her statement. "She's our Star attraction!"

I laugh. "I saw her banner. She must be really good."

"She's our ...."

I hold my hand up and stop her, laughing with her.

"Did you dance with her?"

"I did."

"What can you tell me about her?"

"Nothing."

I tip my head and say. "Now come on."

She laughs. "I'm not at liberty to discuss her."

I slide six chips her way and raise my eyebrows with a smirk on my face.

She takes the chips. "Thank you. That's very generous of you."

"I just want to know how good she is."

She eyes me. "Are you a reporter, a blogger or ...." She stops short of saying it.

"A stalker?" I laugh at that. "Do I look like a stalker?"

She stays serious. "No, but a girl can't be too careful. Why are you asking?"

"It's business, not personal."

She studies me. "An agent?"

"An investor."

"Ah!" She says, knowing that's the truth.

I stand up, pull my money clip out, and find a business card to give her.

She looks at it and says. "She's the STAR attraction because she is unbelievably awesome at what she does."

I chuckle. "Is that the only answer I'm going to get out of you?"

She grins, then says. "I truly can't tell you anything other than that because I don't know anything other than that."

"But you danced with her."

"Yes. I did."

The cocktail waitress returns and I tip her, then ask her. "Who is Surreal?"

She answers the same way. "She's our star attraction."

"Can you tell me anything else about her?"

She says. "No. Top secret." Then walks away to deliver the other drinks on her tray.

I look back to Rebecca for clarification. "Her identity is top secret?"

She looks at me with a confused grin. "Yes. No one knows who she really is. They keep her isolated. They don't even tell the other dancers when a performance is scheduled. We had to be ready at the drop of a hat. It was very stressful for me."

I listen intently, letting her continue.

"Not the dance routine, but not knowing if it was Surreal or the real deal. A screw up or misstep might mean your career, you know? Some of the celebrities are real bitches." She looks at me, wanting me to agree, but the confused frown on my face makes her laugh. "No. You obviously don't know."

"I'm confused. What am I missing here?"

"When there is a 'Surreal' performance," she does quotes with her fingers, "no one knows if the dancer is Surreal or JLo, or Brittany, or Beyoncé."

"Oh! She's an impersonator!" I laugh.

"Yes." She joins me. "You didn't know that?"

"No. I missed that key fact."

"She's an excellent investment if that is what you are wanting to know."

A new player sits down and our conversation ends for several games, then I ask her. "So do you miss dancing?"

"Not really." The other player stands. "I enjoy

dealing and the tips can be just as good." She smiles at him. He smiles back and slides her a chip. She thanks him, and he leaves. She deals another game to me.

"What can you tell me about Seary?" I ask for a hit by touching my cards.

She smirks as she flips one up for me. "She's our headliner."

I smirk back and cover my cards. "Did you dance with her too?"

"Yes. I did and she's the real reason you're asking these questions."

I laugh. "Busted. Tell me about her." Leaning forward I rest my forearms on the table and study her. "Is she any good?"

She laughs. "She's our headliner, of course, she is good." She takes two cards and loses.

When she pushes my winnings to me, I ask. "Can you talk about her?"

"Yes. I can talk all day about her."

"So talk." I tip her two chips, then push 4 more at her. She eyes them, and I lay my hand down on top of them, covering them. "Tell me everything you know about Seary."

She laughs out loud. "She's great! The best dancer I've ever had the pleasure of sharing the stage with."

"What makes her so special?"

"Special? She's not just special. She's unforgettable." I laugh at that over the top analysis and she says. "I'm serious. She is more than a natural talent. She's a phenom." I smirk and she gets defensive. "I'm telling you straight up. Her dance interpretation is so unique!" She looks away, remembering. "It's really amazing the way she lets go, getting into the music and the moment. There is no counting, no thinking, just pure art." She looks back. "Seary is one of those dancers that comes along once in a lifetime." She looks back at me. "You'll get to see her tonight. She's scheduled to dance."

I nod. "I'm looking forward to it. Anything else you want to add?" I look down at the chips under my hand.

She grins really big. "Yeah. She's a real sweetheart too. The kind of girl that other girls love." Her fingers touch her ear and she looks down at the table, then smiles a bright smile. "Your party has arrived and is waiting for you with Beverly."

"Excellent." I push the chips to her and stand. "Thanks for the intel."

"No problem. Stop back by on your way out later."

"If you're still here, I will." I wink at her.

"I want to hear you say. 'Rebecca. You were right. Seary is unforgettable.'"

I chuckle and give her a doubtful smile. "It takes a lot to impress me." Then I turn and walk away to find out for myself if Seary really is unforgettable.

CHAPTER FIFTEEN

Walking up to the entrance of the Gentleman's Club in Been Jammin', I see Bianca and Kip with their arms around each other. They make a striking pair. He is all of 6'5" and 280 pounds of pumped up mass and she is all of 5'8" and 180 pounds of tough stuff. She likes to refer to herself as fluffy, but there isn't anything fluffy about her. She is tattooed, with half a mohawk and piercings that shout alternative lifestyle, 'Don't fuck with me, or I'll fuck you up.' Since I hired her to manage my rental properties, uncollected rents and turnovers have dropped significantly. When she sees me, she squeals and runs to me. I brace myself for impact, and she jumps into my arms, giving me a big crushing hug and saying in her sweet, high-pitched, fluffy voice. "You handsome

Motherfucker! I've missed you!" I look over her head at Kip and he's smiling from ear to ear. I ask her as she drops off and I spank her rear. "Sup, Tough Stuff?"

"You are looking so fly!" She says and hugs me up. "I so desperately need this date night with my men. Thank you, Baby."

We walk arm and arm back to Kip and I shake hands with him while Bianca puts herself between us, hooks her thumbs in our belt loops, letting everyone know that we are both with her tonight and off limits. The two hostesses I met before are gawking at us, but Beverly is cool and professional as she walks up.

"Your table is ready. I'll escort you inside."

I motion for Bianca to go first, but she pushes me to follow Beverly, then I feel her hand slip in mine. I look to find her grinning at me wickedly while she pulls Kip after her. When we stop at the entrance door and wait our turn to go through, Beverly asks. "Did you enjoy Rebecca?"

"I did. I had a good time with her."

Bianca squeezes my hand hard and I frown down at her.

She asks in a hiss rather than a whisper. "Who the fuck is Rebecca?"

I glance at Kip for help. He pulls Bianca to him and kisses the top of her head, while I answer. "Blackjack dealer."

Her eyes are narrow when she mouths silently to me. "Better be."

I laugh at her possessiveness and turn back to Beverly. She leads us into the club and I'm amazed at the size. Quickly getting my bearings, I analyze the floor plan and realize there are multiple clubs inside. This first one is as big as a concert hall, and houses multiple bars, dance floors and a big stage along one wall with the other walls decorated with live dancers inside cages. Beverly proceeds straight through to the sign that reads, "Gentleman's Club." It is just as big, and also has multiple bars and a stage on one wall, but instead of floor space for dancing, it is all cocktail tables with a maze of runways which have stripper poles.

When Beverly stops, we are at the table at the end of the main runway. "Best seats in the house. Enjoy the show." She states simply, then walks away.

Our waitress takes our order, then vanishes. The three of us sit facing the stage. Bianca, naturally in the middle, puts both elbows on the table, folders her fingers and rest her chin on her thumbs. She watches the dancer right in front of us, twirling around the pole. Kip looks at me and nods his head in her direction with a 'check out her intensity' look and I grin back at him. The dancer has some seriously sexy moves and pole dancing will be on Bianca's To Do list next week no doubt.

Surveying the room as the music thumps hard enough to feel, I see at minimum twenty dancers twirling around us on the poles, or bumping and grinding on the runways, and maybe another ten offering lap dances on patrons in the audience. Keeping my eyes averted from the sensual dance happening right in front of our table so my cock doesn't grow any larger, I notice a few girls leading customers off, and I can only assume they are heading to the VIP rooms for a private dance.

Suddenly the whole place literally thumps once with a deafening bass and strobe light, then the room goes complete black. Startled Bianca makes a small yip and sits back in her chair. The room is quiet for a split second, then "THUMP, THUMP. THUMP, THUMP." Scanning the room during the strobe flashes, I see that all the dancers are heading out. In silence, Kip leans over to me and says. "Perfect timing. Seary is about to perform."

I lean over to him. "I certainly hope she's as good as all the hype."

"THUMP, THUMP. THUMP, THUMP.... THUMP, THUMP. THUMP, THUMP." *The timing is a heartbeat. Nice!* The heartbeat "THUMP" continues matching the song cadence as "Sex" by Cheat Codes & Kriss Kross Amsterdam plays. In the strobes, I see ten dancers in only G-strings and pasties pairing up and posing in different sexual positions, then dancing and rearranging their pairs. *Kama Sutra, sweet.*

There is one dancer who seems to be the main attraction. I analyze her quickly. She is blonde, yes, and has a great body, including big tits and nice ass, but she isn't what I was hoping for. She is very good, and her dance skills are superb but definitely forgettable. Still, my dick is enjoying the show. Each loud "THUMP" vibrates it and I put my hands in my lap to stop it.

Our waitress comes up with our drinks and leans over me to place them on the table. Bianca, back in charge, leans forward and practically hisses at her. She smiles at me none the less and I can't help smiling back. I straighten my leg, and reach in my pants pocket, pull off a couple of bills and tip her tits. She grins and leans down to talk in my ear. "I'll be back to check on you, big boy, in a little while."

I nod and she disappears. When I look back at the table, Bianca is glaring at me. "What?" I say innocently and reach for my drink.

I can see her mouth moving but because of the loud music, I thankfully can't hear a word. Kip is clueless. His eyes are feasting on the dancers.

Taking a sip of Crown, I nod my head at Kip. She looks over at him and realizes she isn't the center of his universe at the moment and she turns her attention back on him. Holding my drink in my lap, I steady my cock again and concentrate on enjoying the show without a hard-on.

As the song ends, the dancers lay lengthwise on the stage, head to head and toes to toes, in a single line, and the big-breasted girl that I assume is Seary crawls over them. Dragging her hair and tits over their abs, she tosses her mane, making it hit their pussies, while she twerks over the faces. The sight is sexy as fuck as she moves down the line. Whoever thought that up knows how to insight arousal. The dancer reaches the end and splays out too. The thumping gradually gets softer and softer while the stage and runways slowly illuminate, dimming the effects of the strobes still matching the bass.

I look at Kip and Bianca. She slid closer to him and hooked his arm so her tits are pushing into it. I smile, lean forward and say. "That was hot!"

"Yeah, it was." Kip agrees.

Bianca reaches for her drink. "It was a good warm up for Seary."

"That wasn't Seary?"

"Hell no!" Kip exclaims. "That's the opening act."

"Oh. I didn't realize that."

Bianca grins over her drink and winks at me. "Get ready to get horny, Baby."

CHAPTER SIXTEEN

I look back at the stage and take a sip of Crown. Someone has placed a straight back chair on it and two dancers complete with flamingo feathers stand beside it.

The voice of an announcer booms in the room. "We have a birthday boy in the house. Johnny Robinson, please stand up." The crowd erupts with cheers and clapping as a young man at the table next to ours stands. The announcer continues as the dancers carry the chair down the runway inline with where he stands. "Johnny is twenty fucking one!" More cheers and clapping. "You know what that means!" Chants of "Seary's Hot Chair" start and the announcer says. "Johnny ... if you dare ... take Seary's Hot Chair."

The THUMP, THUMP, THUMP and the strobes

return, but with a different rhythm. Johnny, whose grin is from ear to ear, waves again to everyone, but he shakes his head declining the dare and sits back down at his table.

The crowd yells. "Take the fucking chair! Take the fucking chair!"

Kip leans toward him, cups his hands beside his mouth and chimes in. "Yo, Johnny boy! Take the fucking chair, Brother!"

Bianca rolls her eyes. She leans over and tells me. "He wishes it was him."

Johnny's friends pull him from his chair and push him onto the stage. The two strippers take him by the arms and guide him to his birthday throne. Before he sits, he flips everyone off, and the crowd roars with laughter. Then he plops down in the chair and finds himself promptly tied to it. He leans his head back and I can see the dread in his body language.

The lights go dark again, except for the beam of a direct spotlight on him, and one circling the curtain on the stage. The crowd goes instantly silent as the THUMP, THUMP, THUMP, and strobes take over. Anticipation is heavy in the air. The tension is thick as the excitement builds, then the plucked notes of an electric guitar fill the room, and I recognize "So Contagious" by Acceptance. *Hmm. Interesting choice.*

Kip leans over and shouts. "This is going to be good."

But I don't hear him. The circling spotlight found its target when the curtain was pulled back and a goddess dances onto the stage. I know without a doubt, *this is Seary!* Staring at her, spellbound by her beauty, my mind goes blank and the words of the song think for me. *Wow! This is unexpected!* My cock fills with blood. One hand instinctively seizes it, trying to choke the life out of it, while the other hunkers down on my drink and I struggle to get a grip on myself. She boldly bounces onto the stage to perform for a crowd of drunken fools, but her graceful movement belies her occupation and I recognize a gifted and talented dancer before me. She moves with the elegance and poise of someone who could, and probably should, be dancing on a larger, grander scale. *She is perfection in motion.*

I sit motionless, completely spellbound and locked down tight in my seat, not wanting to miss a thing. Appreciating that every moving part of her beautiful body is in total rhythm to the beat. Right down to the smallest nuance of the melody. *She is incredible.*

Her costume, or rather the lack of, is breathtaking in its

simplicity. She is not wearing a single piece of cloth, but rather she is wrapped in small gold chains. Her skin tone is healthy and natural. Not a fake salon tan, but sun kissed with a faint tint of red. Her tan accentuates the gold chains that reflect the light from the intense spotlight, highlighting her voluptuous body. As she moves and flows, dancing toward me heading to Johnny, her breasts stir my lust even further. They are perfectly proportioned and symmetrical, but they are moving and flowing, bouncing up and down, jiggling out the top of a gold bodice like only natural tits do. My tongue touches the corner of my lip and plays there. The thought of sucking, soft, little pieces of her velvety skin between my lips, to lick then graze with my teeth, draw my balls up tight as they fill with cum.

Little gold chains are wrapped around her long graceful neck and her platinum blonde hair is drawn high in a ponytail that sways from side to side with each strut, held in place by a single gold ribbon. *I know she knows how to do a hair flip that will take your breath away.*

A gold chain G-string and gold stilettos complete her attire. As she mixes her dancing up between erotic and exotic, her body glitters. *When your body is that perfect, there are no flaws to hide.*

I am unable to take my eyes off her, unable to see anything else, and unable to hear anything but the music of her dance as her body literally sings like a siren to me. No woman has ever had this effect on me. *She is simply stunning!*

When she reaches Johnny, she begins to twirl faster and faster, unspooling the first layer of gold chains, slowly revealing more and more of her beautiful, flawless skin. When she stops abruptly, her tits are barely covered, and they rebound from the velocity. The mounds of mass float under her skin in a sexy rolling motion as they come to rest in their proper place. *Fuck! She is stacked and packed.*

She pulls off the gold ribbon holding her hair and shakes her blonde mane out, letting it float like a cloud down around her shoulders. Then she takes the ribbon and twirls it, making it float in the air as she dances under it. Doing a couple of spinning hair flips that does indeed take my breath away.

She is breaking me down. So fucking contagious. Making me ache all over. My gut clenches and I battle my full hard-on throbbing in my jeans.

Then she kneels on the chair, straddling Johnny's lap and hovers over him, dominating him. Her tits inches from his face. The sight of her pussy being spread wide open lights my cock up! I bite my tongue and hold my breath, as a wave of lust racks my whole body.

Then she ties the gold ribbon around his neck and the other end to the chains still tightly bound around her breasts. I swallow hard wanting to see those tits naked. She leans closer to him, dropping her head down so her hair engulfs his face, and I wonder what she smells like in that moment. She lifts her arms like a swan, then drags her hair off his face as she arches away, slowly bending her back, reaching for her heels, tightening the chains as she gets further away. Her hair falls off her tits and hangs down off her head. I'm impressed with her flexibility and that pose sends my mind dreaming of Kama Sutra positions we could enjoy together. When she grabs her stiletto's, the chains bust, letting the remnants of the corset melt down her hard abs, sliding into a pile of gold on Johnny's lap. *He is one lucky, son of a bitch, birthday boy having that gift unwrapped like that.*

Then as she begins arching back up, my gut tightens into a hard knot. Her breasts are bared for all to see. *Fucking A! That is fucking HOT!* Her areolas are painted with gold dust and her nipples are taut! The sight of them makes everything inside me burn hot. My tongue runs quickly back and forth over my lip. *What I wouldn't give to flick those nipples and suck those tits!*

Plump, full, round, soft and firm, they are begging for attention.

When she pushes them together, then jiggles them up, and down in opposite directions, a soft desperate moan escapes my lips. *What I wouldn't give to fuck those!* My cock throbs wanting to be between them. *They are perfect!*

Johnny leans his head down trying desperately to sink his face in them. The thought of him touching her causes my jaw to clench and that primal something that lives just under the surface, dangerously wants me to jump up onto that stage, jerk her off him by her hair, smash my fist in his face, then drag her off somewhere to fuck for as long as I can and as hard as I can, pounding her pussy, gorging myself on her breasts, knowing this time *once will not be enough.*

She drops her tits, puts her fingertips on his forehead and pushes his face away. Then she stands up, spins around and sits on his lap. *Fuck!* Johnny lets out a frustrated roar and tries to get his arms loose. *Thank god, the motherfucker is tied to that chair. If he touched her right now, I would fuck him up, and enjoy it.*

She stands, blows him a kiss, then dances straight to me. Her perfection fills my mind completely. Golden tits freely moving in rhythm with her stride. She stops at the edge of the stage and my eyes devour her gorgeous golden tips. Then she looks down, scanning the crowd and I see her face for the first time. Her eyes are light green and her features are Norwegian. Her lips are a dark soft pink and a wave of passion washes over me. *I wonder what her sweet lips taste like and if her nipples and pussy are the same color.*

She looks out at the darkness to connect with the crowd, yet she is unable to see anyone. She smiles a beautiful smile, full of gentleness, and hope. Her happiness radiates her face, giving her a glow.

She turns away, and my eyes drop to devour her ass. It is as spectacular as the front. She grabs the stripper pole and flings her legs up, pushing herself upside down, she does one complete revolution, then drops into a squat on her perfect ass. Holding onto the pole, she leans her torso away, and lets her pussy bump and grind it. Everything in me wants to feel her doing that to me.

Standing again, she struts away, back to the birthday boy, and I watch her butt cheeks roll as she goes. *They are powerful glutes. Perfect for pounding!*

When she arrives, she does the unthinkable. She takes her shoes off, then puts her foot between his legs, and rubs his hard-on. *Oh fuck! I can feel her toes massaging his dick.* Pre-cum seeps out of my cock. I push it down and shift in my seat. Then she firmly grasps Johnny's chin in her hand, forces his face to hers and leans down. *I can feel her kiss.* Right before her lips touch, she smiles, then turns his face away. She whispers in his ear and he grins big. I image the feeling as the soft flesh of her lips presses into mine, and her sweet breath on my face, as she times her kiss on his cheek perfectly with the end of the song.

The spotlight goes off.

CHAPTER SEVENTEEN

Silence and darkness again fall on the crowd. My senses already tuned in and hyped up, listen to hear for her retreating footsteps, but I only hear the sounds of people shifting in the audience. No one is talking. Then I pick up on the sounds of footsteps approaching and see out of the corner of my eye the same two dancers in flamingo feathers untying Johnny and helping him back down to his table. His friends stand and pat him on the back or knuckle bump him when he arrives. He is all grins. *I know where his dreams will come from for a while. Hell, I know where mine are going to come from, from now on.*

I drain my glass and place it on the table, then I rise and pull my pants down at the knees so my balls, full of cum, can move without being pinched. *I need a bathroom break.*

FINDING HER

THUMP, THUMP, THUMP. The song "Beautiful Drug" by the Zac Brown Band begins as four spotlights from the four corners of the room circle the crowd to the music. Like everyone else I look around, searching for her. Then with the opening words about a death wish, the beams converge at the very top of the stripper pole.

"Wow." I say as the crowd collectively gasps. Seary is positioned at the very top, doing a split in the air and rotating around it.

She has to be in incredible shape to have climbed that distance and how in the hell did she get that red outfit and shoes on? As the song plays about being high, being addicted, needing a hit of love, and not wanting to be saved, she spins, doing various splits. When the words say something about letting her hair down, she flips upside down and drops like a rock, then she clamps down on the pole, stopping with a hard jerk. The words mention hair standing up, and I sit there feeling that effect after watching that daredevil move. *Damn! Fearless.* I stare unable to take my eyes off her and I know everyone in the room is glued to her too. The rest of the song, she owns the pole and the way she moves on it drives me crazy with thoughts of fucking her. *She is so limber and strong. Fuck we could have fun!* When she gets to the landing, she lightly touches down and I know the song is absolutely right. She is "a beautiful drug" and I'm at risk of being addicted to her.

When the song ends another immediately begins. The runways have filled with dancers and they are swaying to the song, "Loved Me Back To Life." Seary in a red teddy and red heels walks in and out of the girls down the runway, making her way to the stage. When she reaches it, right on cue, they all begin dancing a routine, but she is more expressive in hers. I'm enthralled watching her dance interpretation. Her moves make the words resonate in my heart. I can literally feel her bringing it back to life. It's thumping harder for her now than my cock is. When the words say strong hands and an open heart, I imagine my hands cupping her body, holding her tight against me and cherishing her like I have never cherished anyone before, allowing her to see my pain. As she dances, I see 'life' spinning across the stage, then she spins into the curtain and vanishes.

For a moment, I'm frozen, then there is deafening applause. I whistle and stand, clapping as hard as anyone else while the other dancers run off the stage.

I turn back to see Bianca, standing on the chair in front of Kip. She spins around to face him, wrapping her arms around his neck, pulling him tight into her chest as she looks down into his face. He gives me a blind thumbs-up, then puts his hands on her ass and squeezes her butt cheeks.

I have got to go relieve myself. I walk by them and Kip asks. "You good?"

"Yeah. Nature's calling."

"Hurry up. She's not finished and I know you don't want to miss it."

I pat his back as I walk by. "Order me a double. Make it two doubles. I'm gonna need it."

He laughs, and strangely Bianca doesn't say a thing, but I'm too distracted by the cum in my balls needing to be expressed to give it much thought. I hurry away, knowing there is no way I can sit through another round like that and not shoot my wad in my pants. I have got to release the beast.

The floor is lit with soft red led lights and I find the mens room easily. It is full and I wonder how many of them are here for the same reason. I enter the stall, lock it, unzip my pants, push them down so my balls can breathe. I inhale and exhale deep breaths with a slow rhythm as my hand slides all the way up and then all the way down the length of my fully erect cock. As I jerk off, my mind feels crazy as images of Seary flash through it like a kaleidoscope of snapshots through the camera lens. The faster the images spin, the faster I pump until I'm dumping a full sack of my cum into the toilet. The thick fluid splashes as it hits the water in the bowl, then I lean against the side of the stall breathing cleansing air with my cock in my hand wondering what the fuck has happened to me. I shake my head to clear it, but she won't go away. I see her bouncing down the runway again toward me, with her golden tits and her hard nipples front and center and the vision fills my cock again. I want to moan in misery, push her out of my head, stuff a soft dick in my pants, zip it up and walk out, but instead I reach forward and flush the toilet, then start sliding my hand up and down a shaft that is rock hard again, stroking the head of my cock, knowing I need to blow another wad of cum from my balls before the damn beast will fit back in my pants. I close my eyes and her round ass gives my mind the imaginary this go round. Wrapping my fingers around the head of my rod, I jerk the crown hard while I imagine her bent over my bed, her beautiful big butt sticking in the air, while my fucking cock pounds her tight pussy. I open my eyes and watch it disappearing inside my grasp as I envision watching the head disappearing inside those powerful glutes. The sound of my whacking becomes the sound of her ass smack my abs with the force of my thrust and getting close to blowing again, I close my eyes and watch the rippling effect my power has on her butt cheeks. I break a sweat on my lip and brow with the exertion. I have to hold back a moan again, and my knees want to buckle with the exquisite feeling of an over sensitive tip, and I momentarily lose my balance but thankfully the ejaculation hits the target again. When I'm pumped dry, I lean back on the door and suck air in, then wipe the sweat away. My mind is thankfully clear of her fog now. *Fuck! I haven't jacked off back to back like that since high school.* Conscious again of where I am, I flush the commode again, wait until my semen has disappeared, then stuff my soft dick inside my jeans and zip the motherfucker up. I open the stall door and keep my eyes averted, but no one is looking at me anyway.

As I wash my hands, I look at myself in the mirror. My face appears calm and cool, but my eyes tell me a different story. They look bewildered. I splash water on my face, then lean on the sink and stare at my reflection. *I have to face the reality of what this means. Seary has somehow managed to crack through the barrier I locked my heart behind to keep it untouchable from the likes of bimbos like strippers.*

The dude next to me asks, "Hey man, you alright?"

"Yeah. I'm cool. Just drank to much to fast."

I turn away and pull some paper towels off the machine to dry my hands. I throw them in the garbage cans on my out. I glance back at my reflection before I face her again. The same bewildered look is still there.

Dammit. I've fucked up coming here. I hang my head as I push the door open. *She is going to be trouble.*

CHAPTER EIGHTEEN

When I step out the bathroom door, I lean up against the wall and wait, not ready to go close enough to face her again. The lights on the stage are illuminated and my whole body tunes in to find Seary. "Wild Things" by Alessia Cara is playing. Another set of dancers are lined up and dancing, then there she is, sexy Seary. *She is incredible!* My cock thumps acknowledgement when I see her. I watch from this safe distance as they perform a choreographed dance routine. Seary is dancing circles around them. Her advanced talent and skill are obvious to me. This song is so spot on as well. She is a wild thing and making her own way. Bold, confident, and in your face about it too. *I like that!* Listening to the song and thinking about the others she has chosen tonight, makes me realize this woman has depth. She is more than a stripper.

A man exits the men's room, glances at me and leans against the wall beside me. I recognize the birthday boy and say. "Sup?" He gives me a head nod. "So how torturous was that?"

He laughs and shakes head. "Hell! Pure hell!"

I laugh with him. "Everyman's dream and worst nightmare."

He huffs. "That's for fucking sure." We watch Seary on the stage, lost in our own thoughts about her, then he adds. "I'll never forget her as long as I live."

I chuckle at that truth. "So what did she whisper in your ear anyway?"

He grins. "She said in the cutest southern accent. 'I'm going to give you a birthday kiss on your cheek right now, Sweetie. Don't move! I'm warning you. If you turn your face to steal a kiss, I'm going to turn Mr. Rooster down there into Miss Hen. Understand?"

We both bust out laughing.

"So she's not only sexy but sassy too, huh?" I ask him.

"She's got some serious attitude."

"Sexy and sassy is a deadly combination."

"Yeah it is." He stands and I hold my hand out. "Happy Birthday, Brother."

He takes it and says. "Thanks." Then he walks back to his table. I watch him managing the maze, still not ready to return to mine.

When the dance is over, Seary leaves the stage and hoping that that was her last performance for the night, I go back to my table.

When I arrive, Kip tells me the obvious. "Your drinks are here."

"Thanks." I sit down, take one and toss the whole thing back, pick the second one up and do it again, then I slam the glass down. "Ah! That's better."

He whistles. "Damn Aurei. I don't know that I've ever seen you do that."

I give him a 'you're crazy' look. "What are you talking about? We've gotten wasted together plenty of times. Have you forgotten or were you too wasted to remember?"

He chuckles. "Naw man. That's not what I'm talking about."

Oh, that. "What's your point?"

"Nothing." He smirks.

"Had to go take care of business." I grin at him.

He grins back. "Yeah. Nature was calling."

"That's right."

I look at this new quiet Bianca. She is staring at me, disengaged, which is completely out of character for her. "What's in your craw?"

"Nothing."

I realize that's girl code for 'something big,' but I lose focus when the THUMP and strobes bust the air again. *Fuck!* My mind shouts 'no' but the entire rest of me tunes in. I sit there struggling with myself and staring blankly at Bianca. *Could I walk out without a backward glance?* Then the song begins and it's "This Is What You Came For" by Calvin Harris, featuring Rihanna. *The song choice is perfect.*

Bianca moves, and the motion brings her back into focus. She nods to the stage and mouths. "She's on again."

I can't resist. I turn to look at Seary marching down the runway right to me. Tits flowing in all their glory. She has changed her costume. No chains. No strings. She is wearing feathers. Little, tiny, down feathers that cover only her pussy and her areolas. She has white feathers woven into her hair too and the visual effect is that of wings on her back. Blood floods my cock again and a wave of hot desire pulses through me. Knowing the lightening she is creating is going to shoot me in all the right places and knowing my balls are going to be full of cum again before this is over, I slough down in the chair and straighten my legs.

As she moves down the runway, a couple of men stand and wave cash at her in hopes she will come to the edge of the runway to them. Oblivious that she isn't wearing anything that they could stuff the bills in. She skillfully maneuvers out of their reach. Then one drunk dude puts his hands on the stage and attempts to climb up. The knot in my gut and my jaw seize at the same time. Two men snatch him off instantly and take him down. Looking around now, I see men dressed in black, blending in with the audience and I realize how tight her security is. Out of the corner of my eye, the drunken trespasser is subdued and being quietly escorted out.

When she mounts the stripper pole in front of me once

more, she proceeds to do things to it that makes my cock hard and throbbing for her again, and my only salvation is that I just had a back to back jerk-off session less than ten minutes ago. I'm able to study her undeniable talent this time.

Her gracefulness is a thing of beauty. Her timing is perfect. No movement is off. Her arms and legs, hands and feet are pure poetry in motion as she moves up and down its length, dancing sensually on it, arousing thoughts of having sex in everyone here. *She is a real artist.* When she drops to the bottom of the pole at the end of the song, she swings around it, taking a unique bow. The people around me rise, giving her a standing ovation and I stand with them.

As she scans the crowd, waving, our eyes touch and in that flash of an instant, Easy's face flickers in my mind. Shocked, I sit down with my eyes locked on Seary.

The music moves immediately into "Dangerous Woman" by Ariana Grande and she backs up against the pole. Sliding down it, then right back up, she proceeds to seduce the room as she slinks her sexy, sassy self back to the stage, and like everything thing else she has done tonight, her dance and her song choice are spot on, speaking directly to my heart. When she vanishes from sight exactly on the last note of the song, the crowd in the room explodes again with applause, and cheers. I join in knowing one thing is for certain. *I want this sexy, sassy little stripper. I want her staring into my eyes, wearing the look on her face that Easy had.* I smirk. Bold and confident too, knowing I always get what I want, because I make it happen.

CHAPTER NINETEEN

The announcer comes back on and thanks everyone on Seary's behalf. Knowing the show is over, the crowd collectively sits back down and the noise level of intercommunication becomes loud. I look at Kip and Bianca as I turn my chair back around and scoot it up under our table. Kip is grinning from ear to ear at me and I can't help the stupid grin that responds to his. I feel like a school boy who has just gotten caught stealing a kiss from his first crush.

Kip asks. "So.... What did you think?"

"I think you were right. She's as hot as her name implies."

Bianca doesn't say a word and she's not smiling. Her

earlier answer 'nothing' returns to my mind, and I know I need to deal with the 'something big' that is 'nothing.' But the waitress returns and brushes my arm with her tits as she leans in to pick up our empty glasses. "My name is Stacey. May I get you another round?"

I answer. "Yes, please. The same."

When she stands back up, her hip is pressing into my arm and she smiles down at me. "Excellent. I'll be more than happy to hook you up." The innuendo hangs in the air as she continues to hold my eyes and asks Kip and Bianca. "Would you two also like to reorder the same?"

I hear Kip say. "Yes."

"I'll be right back. Don't go anywhere." She tells me, then disappears again.

When I look back at Kip and Bianca, I expect to see her leaning on the table in her usual aggressive jealous position, but instead she is sitting in Kips lap. Surprised, I ask her again. "What's in your craw?"

She gives me a 'really?' look like it's a dumb question and she says again. "Nothing."

Now I give her a 'really?' look and Kip chuckles at us.

"Don't give me that bullshit, Bianca. Something is up with you."

"Not with me. With you."

"What?" I frown at her.

She rolls her eyes. "It's nothing. I'm fine."

"Bianca, we've known each other for years. And in that time, you have never not challenged another woman who is in my presence. What's in your craw?" I stare at her.

"What's in my 'craw' Alabama boy, isn't the question, but the answer is, what's in yours, or rather, who's in yours."

I look at her, thinking about what's she has said, and who she is implying. *Seary. Yeah, Seary is in my craw. First time I've ever had someone in there too.* For just a moment I think about shrugging it off and denying it, but then I realize no point. Bianca's right and she knows she is right. *Wait a minute. Wait just a damn minute!*

"Are you telling me that you've just let it go, like that?"

"No point anymore."

"What the hell?" I shake my head confused by her

certainty. "I haven't done anything different." She laughs with confidence. "Explain yourself." I demand.

She raises her eyebrows at me and I know that was a turn on for her.

"Listen, Aurei. It's the way you looked at her."

I frown, knowing my tongue wasn't hanging out with drool dripping off it. I'm very careful about my facial expressions. I raise my eyebrows at her and command more information.

She looks at Kip for help and he says. "Don't look at me. I'm lost too."

She rolls her eyes like we are children. Stacey comes back with our drinks and again brushes my arm with her breasts as she sets them down. I reach in my pants and pull out a tip for her. She grins as I stick it in her cleavage. "Thanks, Big Daddy."

Bianca says. "You're wasting your time, Hun. He's got Seary in mind."

She laughs and looks at her. "Then I'm not wasting my time at all. She doesn't do extracurricular activities." She looks down at me. "My shift ends in a couple of hours. We can hookup then if you're interested."

I smile at her and ask. "What if I'm gambling?"

"Then you'll need to go ahead and book a room. Let Beverly know you want me."

"Thanks." I smile at her and she turns away, thinking I'm going to. I look back at Bianca. "OK. So, I do have Seary in mind. Why aren't you upset by that? It's not like you to give up."

She laughs. "It's not like me to fight a losing battle either."

I frown at her not sure which direction to pursue with her implications. "Are you telling me if I had brought a date around you, you would have backed off?"

"No."

I frown harder.

"What I'm telling you is the look on your face when you watched Seary, is the same look on Kip's face when he looks at me."

"And what look is that?"

She smiles at me and turns to look at Kip. She kisses his lips, then pulls back and runs her fingers down his temple across his jawline. He looks at her mesmerized. She looks back at me and states. "It's complete commitment."

Her answer startles me. "Commitment? That's a strong word!"

She gives me a soft look that says she's right and I'll discover it on my own.

"What makes you so sure?"

"I've known you a long time and I've pressured you the entire time. You have never given in, not because you aren't attracted to me, and not because you wouldn't dig it, but because you respect our commitment too much. I got that, but I knew I could convince you eventually. This. Her. What I see in your eyes. What I see on your face. That. I will never overcome."

I don't answer. I don't have an answer. I don't know anything right now, except I feel the need to drink. I reach for one of my doubles and slam it down. She and Kip take theirs and Bianca raises hers to me then throws it back. I look at the stage and watch without seeing the dancer on the pole. She does nothing for me.

The three of us sit in silence for a little while longer, then I throw my last shot back and tell them. "I'm going to go gamble. I've seen enough for one night."

Kip pushes Bianca off his lap and stands with me. I shake his hand and he says. "I hope Lady Luck smiles down on you."

"Yeah. Thanks."

"How long are you staying?"

"I'm flying home Wednesday."

"Ok. Let me know if you need anything else."

"Will do." I look at Bianca. She is smiling up at me. Leaning down, I kiss the top of her head, then walk away.

CHAPTER TWENTY

As I exit the Gentleman's club area, I feel like I'm leaving the best thing that's happened to me in a long time behind, unresolved, and it's a haunting feeling. Bianca's words about Seary and commitment weigh heavy on my mind, knowing in my heart she is right. Seary got under my skin, and pierced it. *Sooner or later, I'm going to have to scratch that itch.* My balls and cock jerk confirming they want to lose themselves deep inside her.

Exiting Been Jammin's, I see Beverly sitting at a table alone in the fake patio area. *No time like the present to seize on an opportunity to move forward.* I walk over. She has an iPad and a drink. She looks up when I pull a chair out. "May I?"

"Certainly." She smiles. "Did you enjoy Seary's show?"

"I did. That's what I want to talk to you about."

She sits back in her chair. "May I get you a drink?"

"No. I'm good. Thank you."

"What can I do for you then?"

"I want to book a private meeting in a VIP room. Just me and this girl. One on one."

"Excellent." She sits back up.

"I'm counting on you to make my fantasy come true."

Laughing, she pulls her iPad to her. "I can help you with that."

"There will be a big bonus for you if you do."

"I like big bonuses. Who's the lucky girl?"

I pause for emphasis, making her stop and focus on my choice. Remembering what Stacey said about Seary not doing extracurricular activities and wanting Beverly to know I'm serious, I wait until our eyes connect, then I deepen my voice and answer. "Seary."

She looks surprised and says impulsively. "She isn't available."

I smile with confidence. "You didn't check."

"I don't have to." She shakes her head. "I already know. She isn't available."

I look away, then look back, letting my eyes speak to my intentions. I am determined. No is not an option. "Ask whoever you need to ask, but ask. I intend to make this happen."

Her look is just as determined as mine, but her confidence is not on the same level. "I'll ask, but don't get your hopes up."

"Come on." I sound incredulous. "You make it sound like she doesn't do them. She's the star! We both know she will."

"I didn't say she doesn't do them. I said she was unavailable for a one on one session. She hasn't them since her early days."

"Ask anyway and get back to me, asap." I stand and push my chair back in, then turn and walk away. Seary's body dances in my mind and I realize gambling is out of the question. *I couldn't focus even if I wanted to right now.* I pass the Steakhouse, and the smell draws me in. I'm hungry and need to eat before I get on the highway.

The hostess asks. "How many?"

"One." *Damn. That sounded lonely.*

She sits me at a table in the back for two, facing a couple having a romantic dinner together. I try not to watch them, but it's impossible. With each romantic kiss they exchange or intimate laughter they share, I feel the loneliness of one. While the waiter takes my order, the couple leaves. Sitting there staring at nothing, my mind drifts back to Seary. *She is going to be a force to be reckoned with.*

My Porterhouse steak is cooked to perfection and I eat it all. It sits heavy in my stomach and with the flight, workout, two cums under my belt, not to mention the alcohol, I consumed, I know I need to get home and get to bed. After checking out, I walk through the casino. Rebecca is enthralled in the people who are gambling with her and doesn't look up as I pass. Once outside, I hand the valet my ticket. While I'm waiting, I have a thought, and when he comes back with my corvette, I hold out a $20. "Where's the service entrance?"

He looks down at the tip and says. "I'm new. I don't know." He smiles, reaching for the tip.

I pull it back, and add another $20 to it. "Which side of the building do the employees enter for work?"

He grins and says. "North side."

"Very good. Thank you." I take my key and give him the tip.

"You're welcome. Thank you."

When I leave the parking lot, I hook a left and drive around to scope out the entrance on the north side of the club. It's the parking garage. *Hmm. Without knowing what she drives, and if they have designated spots, that's a bust. No way will I be able to catch her going in or out. Too random.*

I head out on to the highway and turn toward my house. My thoughts swirl around Seary. *Where is she from? Where did she study dance? I thought I was immune to lust, but she busted that myth down and stomped on it. Is Bianca right? Commitment? Wow, what a word choice. Commitment. I guess my focus on her was completely committed. I certainly wasn't aware of anyone else in the room. Hmm. And I am definitely going to commit to fucking her.*

I arrive still lost in my thoughts, park, then head upstairs to take a quick shower and wash off the cigarette smoke before bed. Stripping, I toss my clothes in the dumbwaiter and push the button to send it to the laundry room. My hard dick leads the way to the shower. Turning the water on, I get in, hoping the cold water will shrink my cock and I can get in and out quick. *I'm beat.* Stepping directly under the waterfall, I gasp when the cold liquid hits my head, runs down my chest, and between my legs. *Brrr! That's painful! Maybe I should have jumped in the swimming pool instead.* Shampooing the gel out of my hair, I start to shiver, then the warm water arrives. I lean in, and wash away the suds, being careful not to touch my cock. The cold water worked and it's deflated enough to manage. When I step out, I grab a towel, dry off, then walk naked to the bed, and collapse on it. I'm asleep before I can crawl under the covers.

CHAPTER TWENTY-ONE

My eyes pop open. *Johnny said. 'She said in the cutest southern accent.' She's a southern girl.* I smile and fall back to sleep.

A sexy siren, wrapped in gold threads, sings and dances, calling to me.

I'm hypnotized and walk like a zombie to her. Taking the gold thread she offers me, I pull it hard and she spins like a top. Her hair fans out and the speed of her spinning creates a blurry image, showing off her voluptuous hourglass shape.

Big tits and ass, tiny waist. I moan.

SIRI'S HEART

The thread unwinds and falls silent on the ground.

I stand watching, waiting, hungry to see her gold tipped tits as her spinning body begins to slow down. I feel desperate to bury my face and get lost in them.

Suddenly she stops and stands naked before me. Her tits rebounding, and bouncing against each other.

I reach out to cup them.

She places the end of the gold thread in my hand and my fingers wrap around it. She pulls it, wanting me to touch her.

I try to take a step, but something is blocking me. I look down.

The gold thread is wrapping itself around my legs and is turning into a heavy gold rope.

When I look back at the sexy siren, she has turned into a blonde Wonder Woman. Her face is fierce.

We stand there staring at each other. She is supremely confident and my equal. When she smiles, the warmth floods my body. With a sensuous southern drawl, I hear her telepathically asking me something

Wait. I'm actually feeling her ask my heart.

"How do I make you feel?"

I feel compelled to answer her.

She has tricked me. The heavy gold rope is actually the Lasso of Truth and it's forcing me to honestly acknowledge how I feel about her.

I don't know what this feeling is? I've never felt it before.

I open my mouth and tell her, "You are the most beautiful girl I have ever seen. You are simply stunning."

Her smile fades and I feel what she is feeling. Disappointment that I am no different from the others.

She begins to slowly back away and I try to speak again.

"Wait. Don't go."

No words come out. I reach for her but I am completely incapacitated by the rope. Only my thoughts scream to her to stay. But she is denying me. I watch the confident woman disappear and know she will not give another thought.

When she vanishes from sight,

"NO!" I cry out and sit up in the bed. I look around disoriented searching for her. The coldness of the dark makes me shiver and I lay back, sinking in the loneliness.

Staring at the ceiling, the dream still holding my mind, I lay there and realize I've broken a cold sweat. The horror of that feeling surfaces again, threatening me. I can feel the PTSD button being pushed, I put my feet on the floor and sit up. *Fuck! Fucking fuck!* I stand up and move to the blinds and open them. It's still dark. I turn the light and start to pace. It doesn't help. *I need to run.* Going into the closet, I throw on a pair of boxer briefs, sweat pants, hoodie and Nike's. I run down the stairs, through the front door, and out the gate without thinking of anything but the panic inside me and getting it cleaned out. I run to the end of the drive, hook a right and run to the entrance of golf course. I run until the sun has risen.

My clothes are drenched with sweat as I walk back up to my house. Entering, I hear the sounds of humming coming from the interior. *Maria!* I smile. Tiptoeing, I make my way through the house until I'm standing outside the laundry room, waiting for her to exit so I can scare her. My back flat against the wall, I hear her turn on the dryer. She hums and then I hear her coming towards me. I hold my breath and prepare to jump. As soon as she exits, I grab her and yell. She screams bloody murder and I hug her up tight to me. She slips her arms around my waist, burying her face in my chest and we laugh our asses off.

"Ha! Ha! I got you good!"

"Yes you did, Asshole!" She looks up at me, then sticks her tongue out, pushes me away and walks off. "You stink. Go get cleaned up while I go grocery shopping. I'm going to use you as a guinea pig for a new recipe." She flips me off as she leaves out the side door.

When I first met Maria, she was living in one of my apartment buildings. I walked in for my appointment with the manager and waited outside the office patiently while she attempted to negotiate a deal whereby she cleaned vacant units in exchange for rent. She explained that she had income from a cookbook she had just published, but it would be 90 days before she received her first check. She just needed an extension of time. The office manager explained that Maria would have to sign a new lease in her name and without the money for the deposit and first month's rent, her hands were tied. Maria thanked her for her time, walked out and closed the door behind her. She smiled politely at me, but had tears in her eyes.

I held my meeting and when it was over, I asked for an

explanation of Maria's situation. The manager told me she was a good resident and had lived there for two years while she went to culinary school. She had just graduated and was looking for a job in a kitchen, but hadn't found work yet. She and her boyfriend had had a big fight and he had moved out. The apartment unfortunately was leased in his name. I asked to see the background check on her, then I looked on Amazon and saw her cookbook was ranked in the top 10.

When I knocked on her door, and introduced myself, she invited me in. I was shocked by what I saw. Her kitchen was spotless, and set up like a miniature professional kitchen. She had converted her living room area into a studio. I was impressed with the equipment and knew she took what she was doing very seriously. There was barely any room to move. She asked if I would like a cup of coffee and I asked for a cup of cappuccino instead. She made me one, complete with a heart in the foam, and served some delicious homemade cookies. Before the afternoon was over, I had negotiated a deal with her to be my house sitter in my new house in Red Rock Canyon. She could live in the guest house and use the kitchen in the big house for her video blog.

Watching her walk away, and flipping me off reminds me of the time years ago when she told me she wanted to do my laundry. We argued over it. She was stubborn and insistent, but I refused to think of her that way. "No. We are friends, Maria. You agreed to housesit for me. Laundry is not part of the agreement. Drop it." She snuck up here in the middle of the night anyway to do my laundry while I was sleeping. I heard someone down stairs, creeping around and came down to investigate. At the time, there were no motion sensor lights inside and I stalked the noise in the dark. I located the intruder in the hall, and flattened my back against the wall, waiting to ambush them. When she went by, I hit the lights and pointed my gun at her. She screamed bloody murder and dropped like a rock. I was horrified and thought I had killed her, but she had only fainted. When she came to, I was leaning over her face and whispering. "Maria. Maria."

Her eyes focused on mine and she said. "You're butt naked, Asshole!"

We died laughing and she sat up, then pranced off. Before she left the room, she flipped me off.

Laughing, I enter the laundry room and strip, then head upstairs for another quick shower. The long run helped to clear my mind. Enjoying the warm water, I take my time, thinking about the renovations in the east wing I want to do and specifically keeping my mind off

Seary. I'm feeling great when I go back down stairs to wait for Maria to return. In my office, I turn on my laptop, then go to the drawing table and roll out the plans to review. I like working with my hands and doing as much of the construction as I can. I make a project schedule, a list of subs I will use for what portions, a timeline on completion and a list of what materials I'll need for the entire project, and what I'll need to start.

When Maria returns, I go to help her. I spend the remainder of the day, eating and being her guinea pig for several new dishes, laughing and cutting up with her, teasing her that this taste terrible as I eat every mouthful and then helping her film and edit her clips. We finish washing the dishes together, grab a bottle of wine and go out on the patio to watch the sunset.

Sitting quietly with her, I'm again thankful for my life and comfortable with the way things are. Then Maria starts to talk. "You know, Aurei. Every time I see the sunset from here, the burnt orange glow changing into deep scarlet red on the rock, I think of how passion would look if it had colors. Like a fire that flames orange, then as it gets hotter, burns red until it's so hot, it will scorch your heart no matter if you make it as hard as that rock. You know?" She looks at me. "I miss that. I miss the passion of love." She stands and says.

"Goodnight." Then walks back inside without a backward glance.

I'm left alone watching the passionate sunset and seeing a flame called Seary dance in front of my eyes and I feel the place in my heart she has already scorched. It's warm and feels strangely free.

I wait until the sunlight is completely gone, then I go back into the house, put my wine glass in the sink next to Maria's and head upstairs to change. *I have to see her dance again. Crazy as it is, I have to know if the lust she sparked last night was a fluke or if it was real.*

CHAPTER TWENTY-TWO

I drive my Jaguar to Been Jammin' and get in the line for valet parking. It's long and I sit patiently, thinking about the construction in the East Wing and whether or not I'll go to Italy this year with the family for Christmas or decide to come out here to work on it instead. A limousine pulls past, and I watch with curiosity who is in it. When the car door is opened, I see a pair of stilettos appear and my heart skips a beat. But then I see a redhead exit and my heart goes back to beating normal. I pull up under the canopy and an epiphany hits me between the eyes. *What if she is driven to work and uses the fucking front door? It wouldn't be the first time a club asked their stars to promote their show by allowing the fans close access.*

When the valet takes my information and keys, I ask if the redhead was a star.

"Oh no. Only here. That was Cat. She's part owner, but you never know who will show up. I've opened the doors of limo's and discovered Brittney Spears, Jennifer Lopez and once Toby Keith." He smiles. "Super nice guy."

"That's fly!" I pull a $20 out of my pocket. "Does Seary arrive in a limo?"

He grins at me and winks as he takes the money. "She sure does about two hours before her show starts too."

I enter the casino and walk straight back to the Club. When I arrive at the hostess podium, the hostess politely asks. "Do you have a reservation?"

"I want a reservation," I state and smile.

"Where?"

"The Gentlemen's Club."

"There isn't anything available tonight, but I can put you down for tomorrow night."

I look away, trying not to show my displeasure at having to wait another night. It's not in my nature to let things just happen. It's in my nature to make things happen. "Yes. Please. Put me down for tomorrow night." I give her my name and contact information, then walk away a few feet, stop and walk back up, holding a $50, leaning in and whispering to her. "I forgot to tip you. Excuse me."

"That's very considerate of you."

"If you have a no show tonight on a reservation, please give me a call. I want to fill it. There's a twin in my pocket for you if you do."

She laughs. "If there are triplets in your pocket, I can guarantee we will have a cancelation tonight."

I laugh too. "If you can get me one of those elevated booths in the center before Seary's show starts, there are quadruplets in my pocket for you."

"Be here at midnight." She leans away. "And marks it down on her board."

"We'll see you then." I wink at her and pat my pocket.

Walking away, I feel like a gambler feeding an addiction. Heading back to the entrance, I check the time. It's 9:45pm. She should be arriving in 15 minutes. Sitting at a slot machine close enough to see outside, I watch the vehicles arriving, absentmindedly feeding it $100's and pushing the buttons letting the reel spin pissing money into it. At around 9:55, four big men in suits, arrive and standby just inside the lobby. At 10:00 sharp, a limo pulls up. The big dudes walk and stand post, then one of them opens the door. A small pair of red Converse tennis shoes and distressed skinny jeans appears first, followed by a red cable ribbed sweater that accentuates nice plump breasts under it. Laying on top of the mounds is one thick braided blonde ponytail. The young lady, wearing a ball cap that's pulled down snug shielding her eyes, stands up and exits the vehicle. Instantly my heart goes from zero to three thousand RPM's and my breath gets cut off in my throat. *It's Seary.* I recognize her by the elegant way she moves. The four men casually surround her and they walk as a unit inside. She smiles at the doorman when he speaks to her and waves at him with her fingers.

Impulsively, I hit the cash out button to intercept her path. No plan in mind. Shooting from the hip. I'll come up with something. Bells start clanging and the light on top of my machine starts spinning. I freeze. *What the hell?* I hit the jackpot. *Not now!* I turn back to watch helplessly as her entourage walks by. She peeks around a massive body to look at my machine and I see her smile of happiness. My heart skips a beat and my breath hangs up again. *What a true beauty she is. No makeup and she's still stunning.* Her light green eyes shift to find mine. The winner at the slot. My gut draws up with nervous anticipation, wondering what feeling I will get when our eyes connect, but her bodyguard's stride blocks the direct connection and my eyes trail after her retreating figure. *Her ass looks perfect in those jeans.*

I turn to the lady sitting two machines down and tell her. "Congratulations, ma'am. You just won the jackpot. It's all yours."

She looks startled with my words, then recovers quick. "Thank you! What a nice young man you are!"

As I walk away, I hear her friend add. "What a handsome young man too!"

I close the distance behind Seary, analyzing how her detail proceeds and how they assess the crowd. *They are trained bodyguards. On the lookout for prowlers and possible stalkers.* An older couple waves at Seary, calling her by name, and she waves back, then stops to chitchat and pose for a picture. She slides in-between them and they hug her up tight while one of her goons takes the picture. I circle around to get a better view, but stay far enough away not to be seen. *It's hard to tell if her goons are more for crowd control than safety, but the way their suits are cut, they could be packing weapons.*

They continue without incident and I fall in line behind them all the way to the fake patio at the Club entrance, and watch as she disappears from my view.

Knowing she's here getting ready to perform, sets me on edge and I decide to wait at the bar. Wedging myself between the men crowded around a nearly topless bartender, I order a Crown and coke tonight. UFC is on the screen overhead, and I absentmindedly watch the two dudes grappling on the ground for position, letting my mind go over the details and formulate a plan of action. *I haven't played this game before. Hmm. Do I begin my seduction first? Her team is punctual which means predictable. I could work that to my advantage. Do I get in her path and get noticed? Getting her alone in a VIP room is a must, and the ideal scenario, but if all else fails, I can book a Fucking Fantasy.*

I decide to text Darren while I wait.

I'm at the Club. Bart runs a top-notch establishment.

A couple of minutes go by unanswered. *He's probably asleep.*

And Seary?

I saw her dance last night. Pure magic.

Awesome news!

My recommendation is to invest.

Excellent! I'll let Bart know I'm a go. Do you want in too?

No. Conflict of interest.

Thanks for your help, Buddy.

No problem.

Someone touches my shoulder. I look to see who is sliding up next to me.

"Mr. Moore." She smiles like a cat who just got a bowl full of milk. "Do you need my help getting a table tonight?"

"No. I have a reservation."

She nods. "I've just left Seary's dressing room."

"And?"

"Trust me on this, you won't want to miss a single second of tonight's entertainment." She pats my back.

"And?" I raise my eyebrows for an answer to the real question.

"Look me up afterward. I'll be sitting right over there again tonight when you leave. I have news."

"Perfect."

"Enjoy the show."

"I'm sure I will." I turn my attention back to the MMA fighters bloodying each other up overhead, but I don't see them. *She has good news. Otherwise, she wouldn't have spoken.*

My alarm goes off at 11:55pm and I walk back to the podium with $200 in my hand. The same hostess greets me and says, "Right this way, Mr. Moore. Tara, I'm going to seat him myself. Cover for me."

Tara checks me out and grins. "Sure."

I follow her to an elevated booth just outside the first row of tables. Designed to seat 10 people, the view of the stage is perfect and I give her the tip when she seats me. The room is packed again and the dancers who are on the stage are really good, high-quality talent.

CHAPTER TWENTY-THREE

"THUMP, THUMP. THUMP, THUMP"
The strobes blind me. My abs harden as I get ready to see Seary in action. The correlation with the beating bass and my increased heart rate, plus the throbbing strobes and my cock's reaction to the anticipation of seeing her nearly naked body just a few feet away, aren't lost on me. *Brilliantly played!*

Tonight, Seary doesn't start with an opening act, she dances out onto the stage alone without music. It's powerful and profound. She doesn't have on a stitch of clothes. Her entire body including her hair is painted deep red and dark purple. *Fucking A!*

When the music does start, it's "Wild" by Troye Sivan featuring Alessia Cara. The words seep into my soul as

I sit there watching her mesmerizing dance. Careful not to expose her pussy, she bends, twirls, splits, and dances wildly. I'm guilty like the lyrics say of trying not to fall, and keeping the old protective walls around my heart. But it's hopeless. *I can't turn away. This woman drives me absolutely wild! Fuck! I want her so bad. I've got to have her.*

When the song is over, she stops dancing and stands motionless on the stage in complete silence. A group of four mimes, Jabbawockeez, run onto the stage and begin looking at her. They step closer, examining her with their eyes and mimes. Then they huddle up, talk, look at her, then huddle, then look at her, nod their heads, high-five and break. Two run off and two walk over and take her arms, raise them to shoulder height, then push them over her head. The other two reappear bringing a long pole and a paint bucket and brush. They mime discussing who is going to get to do what and they flip a coin. The two losers pick up the pole, hoist it over their heads, place Seary between them, dip down so her hands can latch on and they lift her off her feet. She hangs suspended. The other two take the paint bucket and brush, arguing over who gets to paint her. In my mind, little increments of time begin to tick off as I realize only her strong grip holds her full body weight. When the two arguing finally get down to dipping the brush in the paint, my heart seizes when it comes out of the bucket. *Fuck! It's the same gold paint she wore last night on her nipples!* My cock floods blood with the memory of those taut tips, dangling right in front of me and my hand grabs it to stifle the throbbing that's started again. The song "Can't Stop The Feeling!" by Justin Timberlake begins to play and the paint brush is held out toward her body. The mimes, holding the pole, dance around so the brush applies paint. They stop when it thins so it can be dipped again in the bucket and the painter can change places with the other one. Each time they stop and become distracted dipping the paint in the bucket, Seary's body begins to dance hanging from the pole. When they turn back to her to apply the paint, she freezes, holding some very awkward poses that demonstrate her incredible strength.

The whole routine is both funny, seductive and powerful. When the song ends, the painters clap their hands together and admire their work. She has a gold stripe the width of the painter's brush that wraps her body. Starting at her hairline and winding down around those plump tits, around her toned abs, around her asscheeks and down one of her muscular legs. Then the THUMP, THUMP, THUMP and strobes begin again and those two run off the stage, but the other two continue holding the pole.

The next song starts, and it's "Scream" by Usher. Seary swings her body for momentum and flips herself upside down onto the top of the pole. She slowly lowers her feet to it, then springs off, flipping and landing like a cat. The two men, look shocked and flee from her. The lights on the stage go dark and the body paint glows. She begins to dance like nothing I've ever seen before. It's like liquid glowing. My entire body clenches. She mimics withering and it looks like rippling water. My mind locks up. Then she's dancing, moving her hips mimicking lovemaking and it looks like waves. Knowing I could do that to her all night long until we would both be screaming, makes me even more determined to possess her to share my skills with her. *We will be good together. What fucking fun we will have.*

Immediately she transitions into "Pillowtalk" by Zayn. I feel her dance interpretation deep inside me and I realize *we are kindred spirits. That's why she's having this effect on me. Sex is a paradise and a war zone.*

The last song of the show is "Hollow" by Tori Kelly. Expressing how fragile she is and wants to be wrapped and filled like a cup because her vessel is hollow, but she longs to be understood. My heart hurts for her and therefore for me. I feel the need to hold her close, cherish her, protect her.

She ends the dance standing in the exact same spot in the exact same silent pose. The mimes return with a big barrel and stand behind her. They start to swing it, then they heave it up over her head and dump all the water in it on her. The paint washes away and she is left standing there naked, soaking wet, bare bronzed flesh, for everyone to see. *Stunning! She is the most beautiful creature I have ever laid eyes on.* Then they lower the barrel down over her, topple it and pick it up, carrying her off. Right at the curtain, she sticks her head out and blows kisses to the crowd. The whole place sounds like a bomb went off when they erupt with cheers.

I leave without looking back to find Beverly, knowing I'll do whatever it takes to fuck this woman, and I will fuck her over and over and over again.

CHAPTER TWENTY-FOUR

"Mr. Moore." Beverly's smile is confident. "Did you enjoy tonight's show?" She pushes her iPad away from her.

"Yes, I did. That body paint was hot as hell."

She laughs. "I thought you would enjoy that. She was being painted when I walked in."

"It was pretty crucial. So, tell me, have they agreed? I'm anxious to meet her."

"No doubt. They want me to discuss a few things with you, first."

I hear Stacey's voice from last night say. *"She doesn't do extracurricular activities."* I brace for impact.

"Seary is our headlining star and tied directly to our brand."

"I understand that."

"Then you understand that she is an extremely valuable asset."

"I do."

"She's someone we must protect as well."

"And? Your point is?"

"If you agree to all the terms, you'll need to also pass a security background check."

I smirk. *They must do this for all her Fucking Fantasy clients too. That's a good thing.* "Ok. I agree."

"You'll need to provide at least 5 personal references as well. We will be discrete and not reveal why we are inquiring."

"I'm ok with that too." I reach into my pants pocket to get a business card. I lay it on the table, and slide it to her. "This is my Chief Operating Officer. She'll be instructed to give you the information you request."

She takes the card and tucks it inside the flap of her iPad. "Seary's time is extremely limited and therefore very valuable. Being our headliner isn't her only obligation."

"Name her price."

"Before we go there, we want you to understand what a valuable commodity she is. She is one of a kind."

"Oh, trust me when I say, I fully understand that she is one of a kind." I smile at her hoping to assure her. She smiles back, but her eyes show she doesn't seem to get my level of commitment, so I add before she continues her 'justification for this price' sales pitch. "I'll pay $100,000 for a private VIP room to be alone with Seary for a two-hour exclusive session."

Her eyes nearly pop out of her face and she clears her throat. "Excuse me?"

"I'll pay $100,000 ... for a private VIP room ... to be alone with Seary ... for a two-hour ... exclusive session."

Her jaw sags slightly, as she looks incredulously at me.

I smirk and add. "Plus if she agrees after our first meeting, I want an additional 2 hours every two weeks."

She blinks rapidly at me clearly not expecting this, trying to decide what course of action she needs to take. "I'll put forth your offer and get back to you."

"I'd prefer you to put forth my offer now."

She studies my face and sees my determined look. "Yes. Ok." She pulls her iPad to her. I watch patiently while she gets her shit together and opens a chat with someone. I shift in my seat so I can read the texts upside down.

She types. *Are you available to chat?*

Yes. What's up?

*I'm with Mr. Moore discussing Seary."

Ah. Standby. I'm in the dressing room.

Beverly smiles at me. "Just a moment."

Ok. Is there a question about the vetting requirements?

No. He is a go.

Excellent. The price is firm. We won't take less. I thought I made that clear.

Her satisfied cat smile returns. *You did, but he has made an offer with other conditions I'm not comfortable approving. I need your okay.*

What is his offer?

He wants two hours alone with her. An exclusive session.

Two hours?

That's correct!

I don't know about that.

He's offering $100k.

$100,000 for 2 hrs?

That's correct.

Standby.

She smiles again at me. "They are discussing it."

"I can read it," I tell her and her smile broadens.

"I believe you've shocked them too."

I smile. "Perhaps you should go ahead and tell them I want to be on a two-week rotation too." She grins and I realize she must be paid on some sort of commission structure.

She types. *Plus he wants an additional 2 hours every 2 weeks.*

You're joking, right?

No sir! Def not joking.

You're impression? Is he a crazy eccentric?

She smiles and looks at me from under her lashes. *He seems normal enough. Didn't bat an eye at the background checks.*

Ask him.

I laugh at that. "Tell him or them, or her, that I'm neither crazy nor eccentric, just very successful at a very young age, very rich, very private and very picky."

She types that in verbatim.

Damn. Ok then. Wasn't expecting this. Shifting things around. Standby.

We smile at each other knowing they are going to make this happen. The thought of two hours in a room with Seary alone makes my cock very happy and while I stare at the iPad waiting for the date. My mind begins to plan how I will fill the room with roses and magnolias for our first session. The scent of natural beauty will fill it. I'll tie it together with a compliment on her natural beauty and my seduction into her mind will begin. As the time ticks off, my eyes drift to stare blankly out at the people surrounding us. I'll wear a tuxedo. All black. No boxer briefs so my cock can be seen without being exposed. I'll have Champaign and dinner catered. I'll focus the entire time discovering who she was, who she is and what makes her tick. No sex, but I will nail her with a kiss at the end of the night that promises firework the next time.

The iPad lights back up and draws my eyes. Beverly looks down and says. "Well, this is romantic, Mr. Moore. The first available is Valentine's Day."

I can't control my outburst. "Are you fucking kidding me?"

Her eyes are startled with my outburst.

"No, sir. That's what the date is." She spins her iPad around so I can read it myself.

"That's three months from now!" My shock heightens my tone.

"Yes, sir. It is." She apologizes. "That must the first available date. She is extremely busy and we do have the Holiday season coming up. I know many girls take vacations during the month of January too. I'm not sure about Seary, but perhaps that's why." She offers to calm me.

"Ask if a shorter time is available sooner." I point to the iPad. As she spins it back around to ask, I add. "Same price." *That should work. Perhaps they are only negotiating now.* I lean my arms on the table, anxious for the answer. My heart is holding my body hostage.

Offer my apologies, but that's the first available day she doesn't have anything booked. She's a workaholic.

I stand up and my chair almost tips over. I command her to "Book it!"

CHAPTER TWENTY-FIVE

Walking through the casino heading outside to get some fresh air, I see only the floor directly in my path, hear nothing but my own blood pounding in my ears and my own thoughts circling inside my mind.

Seary. Three months. Fuck! My mind is reeling. *How am I going to make it three months?* The thought of returning to Italy to my studio to satisfy my sexual needs passes through it, but only for a fleeting moment. I know I won't be back there until after I've satisfied myself with Seary and that might be a while. If ever again. *Seary has changed everything for me.* Incredible as that sounds, I hear the truth of it in my heart and in my soul.

I exit the door and keep going past the valet station

down the drive. I hook a left and walk. My pace is fast and determined. Weaving in and out of the flow of people, I head nowhere in particular. My mind is tormenting me with the images of her red, purple, golden glow. *The way she looks. The way she moves. Her body. Her dance. Three fucking months. I have to wait three fucking months! I've finally found the one woman who has set my heart on fire and lit a flame burning inside me like I have never experienced before. Awakening feelings that I feared I was incapable of feeling.* I laugh out loud at the irony of the whole thing. *Right when I acknowledge that she could be the one, she's pushed out of my grasp. But I will wait with the patience of a hunter.* I vow to myself.

"LEAVE ME THE FUCK ALONE! OR I'M GONNA FUCK YOU UP!"

I stop and look around. I've walked five blocks North without realizing it. The building I just passed is an abandoned warehouse I purchased a year ago, but haven't renovated yet. In the low light, I can just make out two men squared off between the building and the adjacent vacant lot. There looks to be a makeshift tent to the right under some trees.

"Old man, you ain't gonna do nothin' but give me what I want or I'm going to take it from you."

"What do you want?" I ask as I head in.

I notice three dudes dressed in dark clothes wearing hoodies pulled up over their heads standing behind the young thug, leaning against the building. As I get closer, alert to my approach, they push off and stand up. They are big, but young punks.

"Mind your own damn business." The old man says without looking at me.

"Yeah. Mind your own damn business." The younger man agrees.

"I am minding my own damn business. I own the damn property you're standing on."

That revelation makes them all stop arguing and turn towards me. "What do you want from the old man?"

"They want my special forces ranger knife." He smiles at them. "But I ain't part'n with it."

"How about you give it to me."

"Why the fuck would I do that?"

"'cause they can't take it off me."

"They can't take if off me either."

I walk closer. Going slow to keep everyone calm. I'm

guessing this is a gang initiation. The young men eye me and I stare them down. They are confident that four on one or four on two are odds they can win.

"Give me the knife, old man. I got your back." I hold my hand out for the knife, and all hell breaks loose. The old man turns it on me and lunges. I sidestep him, grab his forearm, twist it behind his back and take it from his fingers. Then I shove him to the ground, step over him and confront his assailants. With a deranged grin on my face, tossing it nimbly from hand to hand, I dare them to be brave. It is equally balanced and feels like my buck knife in my hands. "You think accosting an old man, makes you a gangsta? It only makes you a coward. You think 4 on 1 is good enough odds? Bring it on." I sniff the air. "Ah! I miss the smell of sweat, fear, panic and fresh blood." They all stop as one, realizing I'm dead serious about that. *Punks!* I flip the knife end over end, grasp the blade, bring it by my ear, cock my arm, flip my wrist, step to my target and fling the knife with all my force. The loud thud it makes when it hits and the vibrating sound it makes as it settles down inside its new home, draws everyone's eyes to the tree. Everyone but mine. As soon as I released the knife, I closed the distance on the ringleader and I smash my fist in his face. Before he can fall to the ground, I've hit him two more times. He's out cold when he lands and it's the second loud thud the punks hear. They turn their eyes big as moons on me and I smash my fist in the face of the next closest one. He wobbles but doesn't go down. I shove him out of the way while I step over the unconscious body and draw my fist back to attack bully number three. He steps back, turns and runs after bully number four. "You better run, you worthless piece of shit!" I yell after them, then look down when something grazes my leg. Bully number two is dragging the leader out from under me. I stare him down and he says. "Yeah. I learned my lesson. Don't fuck with old folks."

"I saved someone's life tonight. It might have been yours." I tell him. "Old soldiers don't go down without a fight. Some of us even enjoy them, but others play to win no matter the cost."

He looks past me at the old man who is walking to where his knife is in the tree. Then he squats down, puts his buddy on his shoulder then carries him to the street. I hear the rumble of a car coming down the road and hope this doesn't turn into a drive-by shooting as I walk to the old man.

"You a Seal or something?" He asks me.

"Nope. Just an Army Aviator."

He laughs. "Damn. Fly boy! Thought you were a real soldier."

I laugh with him. "Marine?"

"Oorah!"

He holds his hand out and I shake it. "Thanks."

"You're welcome. It looks good there. You should leave it."

"Yeah. I think it's safe there."

"You got food tonight?"

"I ate at the shelter."

"Alright. I hear they are good people."

"Yeah." He pats me on the back. "Thanks again."

"Sure." I turn around and head back. My mind is clear and the tension along with the frustration is gone.

As I walk, I start making my plans. *I may not be able to taste Seary's sweet southern sexiness for three more months, but that won't stop me from preparing for a long-term fucking arrangement with her. I've got changes to make to the East Wing of my house.*

CHAPTER TWENTY-SIX

The jet touches down and I stretch, smiling. I text Maria. *Just touched down. Be there after I visit the Club.*

Have a good time. We're having Black Barbecue Pork Chops. Don't be late.

Yum!

Leaving the airport, I drive straight to Been Jammin'. When I arrive, Jimmy recognizes my Jag and positions himself to park it for me. When it's my turn, he opens my door. "My man, Moore. You're here early."

I step out. "I'm here to ensure everything is ready for tonight."

"Tonight? You mean tonight's the night?"

I chuckle as I hand him my keys. "Yes, it is."

"Are you finally going to tell me who?"

"Nope." My smile feels like it's brighter than the sun.

Walking through the casino, I head for Rebecca's table. She smiles a warm greeting when she sees me approaching. "Aurei, are you nervous?"

I sit down at her table. "Nervous? No. Excited." I give her my Been Jammin' card and she swipes it, then slides it back with a stack of chips. I gamble at her table while we visit. "Has everything been delivered?"

"Last time I checked everything was here and the crew was setting it up." She grins. "I don't know anyone who deserves each other more than you two. You're both fucking awesome and I hope, no, I know you two will hit it off together."

"You haven't told anyone?"

"Nope. I've kept your secret. I asked around and no one knows who's going to be entertained in the room tonight." She laughs. "No one suspects it's Seary, so she hasn't told anyone either."

"Thanks. This should be epic."

"I can't wait to tell her I've kept your secret all these months and helped you plan it."

"I really appreciate your help making this come together."

"No problem. I'm glad I could. Are you going in to see the room before time?"

"No. I think I'll wait too. So, how's your love life? Any special plans for tonight?"

She smiles. "Monty says he's got a surprise for me. I told him this morning that just waking up beside him was the best Valentine's Day gift I could have received, but he says he has something special for me. Not to work late."

"Any idea what it could be?"

"No and I love surprises so I didn't snoop around before coming to work either."

"Have you gotten him anything?"

"I saw this sexy teddy yesterday window shopping. I'm going to stop by on my way home and pick it up."

"He'll like that." I grin at her.

I play several more hands of Blackjack with her, but I can't concentrate. The man sitting next to me says. "Dude. You seriously should consider a new dealer. You're losing your ass here."

"That's a clue to get out of here," I tell them, then slide my chips back. "That's your tip, Rebecca."

"Aurei. I'm speechless." She tells me with tears in her eyes.

I stand up, give her a wink and tell her. "A small token of thanks. Happy Valentine's Day."

"Oh my gosh. You're the best!"

Driving to the house, I reflect on all the different shows I've watched Seary perform over these three months. My favorites so far were the Holiday ones.

On Christmas eve, she gave Santa a seductive lap dance that had me holding my cock the entire time. Then someone read a sexy version of the Night Before Christmas and she acted the whole thing out. She ended that night with Santa coming down the stripper pole while she was hiding under the tree. When he set about putting presents under it, she started being naughty and causing mayhem. He kept blaming the other dancers dressed like elves and spanking them. It was both hilarious and a real turn on too.

On Christmas night, she did a gift themed dance dressed in bows, peeking in and out of the presents. Opening them to reveal other dancers. The night ended with everyone on the stage singing, "We Wish You A Merry Christmas" as fake snow fell from the ceiling. It was spectacular.

On New Year's Eve, I watched her exit her limo, but she didn't dance, and I roamed all the different Clubs hoping to catch a glimpse of her. It was packed that night, and Jennifer Lopez was rumored to be in the house dancing. I walked through the whole casino with the song by Sam Hunt, "Take Your Time" playing in my head. If I would have stumbled upon her, that was going to be my plan. Security detail or not. Somehow I was going to make eye contact with her and draw her to me. Then I would let her know that I don't want to change her life. I just want some of her time. I grin. *I get to tell her that tonight.*

On New Years Day there was another birthday boy in the house celebrating his 21st birthday, and while she again wore the gold chains and had him tied to Seary's Hot Chair, her dance was entirely different. The only thing similar was the unwrapping of the chains with her as the birthday gift, and those beautiful nipples painted with gold dust. My cock stayed hard the entire night, and in bed, I again dreamed the Wonder Woman dream. Only this time, she knelt in front of me and sucked my cock dry before disappearing. I woke again screaming, "NO!" But I wasn't in a bad place. No panic. Just frustration and sheets soaked with cum from my wet dream.

CHAPTER TWENTY-SEVEN

I arrive at the house and the delicious smell of Maria's cooking. She's in the dining room, setting the table for two when I come in. "Yay! You're here on time!" She sounds more enthusiastic than usual to see me. "Go wash up and let's eat. I have a date!"

I stop dead in my tracks. "A date?"

"Yes!" She claps her hands together, then starts to happy dance back to the kitchen.

"With who?" I frown and follow her in.

"With a man I met at the grocery store." She giggles. "A tall dark, handsome man too." She fawns over his imaginary face. "Oh hell yeah."

"What's his name?" I demand.

She stops suddenly realizing I'm not happy for her. "None of your business." She puts her hands on her hips and sasses me. "Don't go getting all territorial on me now. I won't have it."

"Maria. I. I. I'm happy for you. It's just as long as I've known you, you've...." Her face makes me stop. "I should stop talking now."

"Yes. You should."

"At least tell me where you are going?"

Her eyes narrow, suspiciously. "We're going to his place."

I open my mouth to protest and she sticks her hand out then cuts her throat with it. I close my mouth, but narrow my eyes at her too. We stare each other down. A war of wills. I speak first. "I could tie you up and keep you here."

She bursts out laughing. "He owns the grocery store. I've known him since the first day I moved out here and went shopping to feed you. His name is Trent Monty. He's thirty-three and a real nice man. Recently divorced with three kids. All of whom will be with us tonight. We're going to take them to the UNLV

Runnin' Rebels basketball game. I'll be home before you, but if I'm not, don't wait up." She flips me off as she dances back to the stove.

The rest of our visit is spent eating and talking about our prospective dates. Up until tonight, I had not shared with her who I was going to see every evening these past few months while I was here. When I told her, she whistled and said, "'at a boy! As long as I've known you too, you've never once mentioned anyone either. I knew whoever it was, was someone really special. The renovations to the East Wing are very nice. So how did you two meet? Tell me about her."

I laugh, embarrassed. "You probably know more than I do about her. I haven't actually met her. Tonight's going to be the first time."

She drops her fork. "You've been stalking her?"

"Stalking is a harsh, scary word, Maria." I frown at her and smirk. "I saw her dance back in November and she completely captivated me. I fell hard for her then and made this appointment. I've been watching from the audience and waiting patiently for her for three months. Three long agonizing months."

She laughs with me. "I fell for Trent the first time I saw

him too. I've been stalking him for fucking years. Talk about frustrating patience." She rolls her eyes.

I pick up my wine glass and hold it up. "To our new flames."

"May they scorch themselves forever on our hearts."

When we are finished eating, we clean the table off together, and I push Maria out of the kitchen, then stand blocking the door. "I'll do the dishes tonight. You get going."

"Ok." She giggles. "No arguing here. Even though I know you're going to put them in the dishwasher."

"That's right! Now go!"

I watch her nice ass as she struts out and I call after her. "Wear your skinny jeans." She spanks her ass without looking back.

I go into the kitchen to load the dishwasher. As I work, I start to sing "Fix" by Chris Lane. I'm going to whisper in her ear. "Baby Girl, I'm what you've been missing. I got your 'fix' right here." Then I'm gonna ignite in her a flame that won't go out, make her burn for me. I'm going to make her addicted to me. *Umm hmm. I have big plans for this one.*

CHAPTER TWENTY-EIGHT

In the shower getting ready, I let my mind play all the visions of Seary's expressive passion as she dances that have scorched themselves onto it. *All these months of watching her. I do feel like a hunter stalking its prey, but in a good way; in a very good way. Soon my arms will be holding her tight. My fingers feeling the soft, subtleness of her tenderness. My eyes seeing the yearning in her eyes for me. My body feeling her body withering under me. My ears hearing her moans and calling my name as she begs me to possess her. Then moaning as I own her completely, pounding my cock with hard, hammering thrusts until I shoot my cum deep inside her, marking her as mine!* I step out of the shower and my hard cock leads the way. I grab a towel, dry my hair, then my body and go into my dressing room. My black tux is waiting for me. Getting dressed, I see my reflection in the mirror and stop to stare. I have a shit eating grin from ear to ear on my face. *Ha! I'm so fucking happy right now! Finally!*

I dance out to the garage, slide behind the wheel of the corvette, crank it up, and squeal the tires as I peel away, feeling young and carefree. *In just one hour, I'll be staring into her eyes.*

When I arrive, Jimmy trots out and opens my door. "Mr. Moore. You're back and looking very dashing."

I laugh at his choice of words. "Prince Charming dashing?"

"Yes, sir!"

"Excellent." I give him a nice tip and strut my swag ass through the door, heading to the Gentlemen's Club. When I arrive, I go straight back through the dance hall, which is loud and packed to capacity for Valentine's Day, to the VIP area and swipe my card at the security door. The little green light shines, and I turn the handle. My nerves are raw and I take a deep breath. Entering the hallway, the silence is comforting as I walk down the corridors to find room number 40. Beverly promised it was the largest and had the best acoustics. When I put my hand on the door handle, I hold my breath while I turn it then push it open. The smell of roses and magnolia's hits me and I smile. "Perfect!"

Once inside, I'm ecstatic about the setup. Rebecca has done a fabulous job! There are red, purple and gold silk drapes, hanging on each wall like veils. In the corners are stripper poles, with the fresh flowers woven like vines. In the center of the room is a small table, with a purple silk cloth, ruby red dinnerware and gold tableware. The ice bucket contains a bottle of Moët & Chandon Dom Perignon White Gold Champagne. There are only two chairs in which to sit, tucked under the table. No couch. I wanted to eliminate the temptation for fucking from the room. For these first two hours, my intention is to seduce her only and leave her wanting Moore. I grin. If she wants to return with me tonight to Red Rock, the East Wing is finished. I'm ready for her.

I check my phone. I have only 5 minutes left. One last time, I review the list I prepared, going over what I want to do. *To kiss her hand. To whisper my name in her ear. To watch what makes her smile. To listen to her voice inflections. To watch her mouth move as she talks. To read her body's language. Her pulse beating in her neck. Her breasts rising and falling with her excitement. The way her facial expressions flicker with my words and tone. To drink in her light green eyes and seduce her with mine.*

I take up post by my chair to wait. I'm ready.

....

....

....

What the fuck? I pace in the room. *Something isn't right.* I check my phone. *It's 10 minutes past the hour, but it feels like an hour past.* Then I hear a tap on the door. My first instinct is to say, "Come in." But I know Seary would have. She wouldn't have knocked. My heart locks down tight. I feel cold hardcore steel wrapping around it, then I hear the pounding in my ears, drowning everything else out. With deep measured intakes and forced exhales of breath, I gain control, containing my response. I know the pain is coming. I walk in slow motion to the door and watch my hand reach for the handle. The click of the door latch releasing sounds like a gunshot. Pulling it open I stare into the face of Beverly. Her first words confirm my fear. "Mr. Moore. I'm sorry to inform you, but there has been a family emergency earlier today and Seary has returned home."

I close my eyes as I step back and she enters the room. Behind my eyelids, I see the fire burning on the stage of the dancer that has scorched my soul and know, for the time being, she remains untouchable.

EPILOGUE

Leaving the flight line, I check my iPhone for any new messages, but there aren't any.

Beverly's weekly update is late.

Walking back to debrief my students, I wonder. Is no news good news? It's been over a month since Seary vanished.

That night when Beverly explained that she had had a family emergency earlier and had gone home, I was crushed, but not defeated. Beverly assured me I would be the first to know when she returned. I'm back in hardcore survival mode with my heart on lockdown until I see for myself that gorgeous golden goddess again. I refuse to give up hope that she will return to Vegas, and to me.

Rebecca was right. Seary is unforgettable, but I'll be damn if she will remain untouchable. I finally find a woman who makes me feel something and I'm not letting her go. It's not a matter of if, but a matter of when I will have her.

Dos Gringo's song, "Has Anyone Seen My Wingman?" starts to play and my phone vibrates as a call comes in from Dirk Sam. I let it go to voicemail. I know why he's calling. The crazy Brit bitch has decided on which apartment complex she wants to live in. I'll handle it on my way to work in the morning.

Pulling into the parking lot, I turn the key in the ignition and shut my truck down. My eyes scan the landscape. It's a nice, high-end apartment complex. Upscale and quiet. I pick up my ringing phone as my eyes focus on the office building.

"Moore speaking. Yeah man, I'm at Dogwood Court now checking on the apartment for you...." The office door swings open. A bolt of lightning shoots through me and I stare dumbfounded. "What the hell?" My hand lowers the phone and I grip the steering wheel as I stare out the cab at the most beautiful girl in the world as she casually walks across the parking lot right in front of me. I hear Sam talking, and lift the phone. "Let me call you back."

I can't believe it! Seary! Seary is here. Right there!

My eyes follow her like a hawk hunting its prey. She is dressed in a white button-down shirt with a business jacket that hangs open over a matching short skirt. She looks professional, but there is no hiding her curves. Her breasts pushed up by her bra, strain the buttons of her shirt and the cut of her skirt hugs her nice ass. There is no hiding a body built like that. She IS simply stunning!

She stops next to her car, a customized Shelby GT500, and accidentally drops her keys. With her back to me, I watch as the flexible dancer slowly bends over her stiletto's. Her skirt sliding up to hug her perfect ass as she reaches down to them. She takes a small step to the side to balance herself as she reaches under the car to retrieve them and she flashes me.

She is panty-less! I laugh out loud at my view. "This girl is perfect!"

Another lightning bolt jolts me and the word 'perfect' echoes around in my mind, taking on a completely different context, as I watch her pull her skirt down then lower her voluptuous body gracefully into the car.

She glances my way as she eases out of the parking spot and a ray of sunlight highlights her face. "She is simply stunning" falls off my tongue and out my mouth again as I watch her drive away. When she vanishes out of my sight, my gut tightens and I know I *have* to have her.

I close my eyes and lean my head back, absorbing what just happened. I see her dancing on the stage. I feel the fire she lights within me, scorching my soul. Her golden tips, swaying so hypnotically. I open my eyes and stare at the ceiling. My heart has come alive with feeling again and my whole body fills with longing for her. I know I need her like I've never needed a woman before.

I hear Grandpa Al's voice. "You will find someone, Maximus, who can handle your secrets." Then Grandpa Moore's, "Your grandmother completes me, son. She makes me whole."

What if this woman, who has this extraordinary effect on me, is the one who not only can handle my secrets but who will complete me?

I look down the drive where Seary vanished.

And what are the odds that our paths would cross right here, right now? They are truly astronomical.

I grip the steering wheel and hang my head, struggling to think logically.

Only a fool would let a woman like that slip away twice and only a fool wouldn't take advantage of an opportunity like this that has fallen into his lap.

I lift my head and stare at the vacant parking spot. "I'm no fool. I am going to make this happen!"

I open the truck door and get out. As I walk to the apartment building, I call Dirk back. "Sam-I-Am, sorry about that, but the girl of my dreams just walked by."

ACKNOWLEDGMENTS

To my children, whose patience and critical input helped me stay the course. To them, hugs and kisses, always!

Special thanks to my BFF, Cathy Jo, who listened to the raw storyline and helped with the creation of the final plot.

To Carrie Dunn, my #1 fan, literally, who volunteered to read a story from an unknown author, and to BSM Stoneking, who befriended me on twitter (#NaughtyMisfits), read the unedited mess, then offered her honest critique. A thousand years of thank yous! Without you two, I would never have pushed the publish button.

To Maria Clark, End Solutions Inc., who edited the finished product. A big shout out. THANK YOU! You single handedly saved my career!

To Lainey Da Silva, my twin from across the pond, I am forever grateful to you for all you do on my behalf! You are more to me than a fan, or friend. You are family.

To Romance Devoured, you've added so much to my career! I have no words. And that's really saying something!

To Give Me Books for their professionalism and promotion, WOW! Just WOW! Thank you so much!

To my Diva Den, you gals always have my back. I know on good days and hard days, I can pop in and be real with you. THANK YOU!

To all the bloggers, reviewers, and readers - THANK YOU for choosing my love story. There are so many wonderful romance books available. It's easy to get lost in the noise. Without you, the world doesn't turn. I'm grateful beyond words for your time.

To my fans, I want you to know I love and appreciate

each and everyone of you! I am humbled by your love, loyalty, and support! You complete me!

And last, but certainly not least, to YOU! Thank you for reading my book. It's the most amazing feeling, giving others 'happy faces' from a story that comes from the depth of my soul. My goal with every book is to make you sure you laugh out loud at least one, and give you more than one happy ending. ;) I cherish each of you and our time spent together inside my fictional fantasy world. I hope this is the beginning of a long and loving relationship.

Before you go, may I ask you to do me a big favor?

If you've enjoyed Finding Her, please consider leaving a review. Reviews are the lifeblood of authors. They really help others find my books. Thank you!

Ciao!

ABOUT THE AUTHOR

JessikaKlide.com

Jessika Klide is an Amazon Bestselling Author with fans in over 25 countries.

In 1981, she married her high school sweetheart. He is not only her soulmate but her best friend. He is a former Army Aviator, and they are living their Happily Ever After in Alabama.

Jessika Klide also writes as Cindee Bartholomew. Both write strong alpha men who love their strong independent women. Jessika writes scorching hot romance with all the details, while Cindee writes steamy, seductive romance. She believes lust and love form perfect unions and the stars really due align for true love.

bookbub.com/authors/jessika-klide
amazon.com/Jessika-Klide/B00NH7YOA0
facebook.com/JessikaKlideRomance
twitter.com/JessikaKlide
instagram.com/JessikaKlideAuthor

When the obsessive **Aurei Moore** discovers the untouchable Vegas star **Siri (Seary) Wright** in Alabama on his turf, he recognizes a unique opportunity to make the dancing diva his lover on his terms, but he knows he must keep his identity secret or risk being labeled a stalker.

After returning home for a family emergency, the isolated high-value entertainer, Siri Wright, meets a beautiful Golden God with gorgeous green eyes. Shocked by the chemistry that sparks between them, she sets about learning more about her mysterious new neighbor, Mr. Moore.

A torrid affair begins!

Read *FREE* with *Kindle Unlimited!*

ALSO BY JESSIKA KLIDE

Falling For His Badass - Releasing 10/2/19

Amazon, Barnes & Noble, AppleBooks, Kobo:
Preorder Sale: $.99 - Release Day Amazon
Retail: $3.99 / Kindle Unlimited

Lizzy has terrible luck with men.

It's not that she doesn't attract good guys, she does. It's that she settles for "decent" ones.

Tired of making the wrong choices when it comes to men, Lizzy trusts her best friend, Tara, to take her away for the weekend. Lizzy knows that if she wants an all-consuming love, she's going to have to take a bigger risk to attract a different type of man.

But this road trip will yield dangerous results. Her panic button will be pushed, and before the first night is over, she will be falling for his badass.

A Standalone Second Chance Romantic Comedy

When college graduate, Farrah Ford, takes a summer job at Do Donuts, she is pretty sure she has encountered the love of her life. The problem is she isn't sure who he is.

Is he Cade, the sophisticated hot doctor in his 40's who is a regular at Do Donuts and comes in daily to flirt with Farrah?

She doesn't recall meeting "Frosted Stripes", yet she knows she has because his confident demeanor is dominating.

Or is he Justin, the 26 year old, sensual stud fresh from the Navy, who enters the bakery pre-dawn, ties on an apron, rolls up his sleeves, and turns on more than the fryers!

The way "Celebration Sprinkles" dunks his donuts in milk, then eats them, gives Do Donuts a delicious meaning.

So what's Farrah's donut dilemma? She has no idea which dude she is secretly texting!

Read *FREE* with *Kindle Unlimited!*

FREE Download! *https://claims.prolificworks.com/free/vqKbSbds*

A Second Chance Older Man/Young Woman Standalone

At twenty-seven, Vicki had it all. She was a successful Broadway dancer, living the dream in the Big Apple. But when her mother became terminally ill, Vicki left it all behind to go home to cherish the woman who sacrificed everything for her to live her dream. Upon her death, Vicki promised her mother she would dance again, but her heart no longer desired fame and fortune. Now she merely wants to open a dance studio to share her passion with little princesses.

When Nik was thirty-eight, he had it all. A loving wife, a beautiful daughter, and a successful career as an MMA fighter. Four years later, he is a widower with a traumatized princess, and a gym to run. Still haunted by his wife's last word of encouragement "Dance," Nik tries to ease his pain by renovating the dance studio next to his gym.

When Vicki dances into Nik's life, is fate finding a way to fix their misfortunes? Make sure you have some tissues. This love story is a tearjerker.

A Second Chance Standalone Romance

When I arrive in London, I'm on a mission. I have a three day pass from my military assignment to find the woman I will never stop loving and to explain why I left her without saying goodbye six years ago.

I pray she will forgive me. I want her in my arms again. I want my lips on her lips again. I want my cock controlling her moans again.

My mission is to claim what's mine. Her name is Piper Wilson....

Read *FREE* with *Kindle Unlimited!*

On Sale: $.99

A Holiday Novella

Zane Lockhart is a coldhearted, selfish Las Vegas cop who hates Christmas and proudly owns the nickname, Sergeant Scrooge. Refusing to celebrate it in any way except the bellowing of "Bah Humbug," he insists, "it's just another day."

On Christmas Eve, while on patrol with his new partner, a K9 cop named Bruce Wayne aka Batman, he has a chance encounter with a hot chick and sets up a midnight date with her. Off-duty and ready to score a hookup, the two are getting acquainted when Zane comes face to face with a past full of scars, a present full of secrets, but a future full of hope.

Then a robbery occurs....

This Christmas discover that real heroes are born not trained, that "Bah Humbug" can be weaponized, and that love is truly magical!

Made in the
USA
Lexington, KY